George Johnston and Charmian Clift are two of Australia's best-known and loved authors; their colourful and tragic lives assumed almost legendary proportions before their untimely deaths within a few years of each other.

Meeting at the end of World War II, they were unable to settle to a routine existence in Australia and set off for Europe, determined to live by their writing. With their three children, they spent fourteen years in England and the Greek islands. During that time they were a focus for Australia's expatriate artistic community.

They returned home with a string of published short stories and books behind them, including two they wrote together, *High Valley* and *The Sponge Divers*; Charmian's *Mermaid Singing* and *Peel Me a Lotus*; and George's *My Brother Jack*, which he extended into a distinguished trilogy with *Clean Straw for Nothing* and *A Cartload of Clay*. This trilogy has ensured George Johnston's permanent place in Australian literature.

Garry Kinnane was born in Melbourne and had a variety of jobs, from stripping cane to playing the guitar, before leaving Australia in 1964 to live in Greece and England. He graduated BA (Hons) from the University of Warwick, and M. Litt. from Oxford University, before returning to a senior tutorship in English at Monash University in 1974. He is currently a lecturer in English at Ballarat College of Advanced Education, and is writing a biography of George Johnston.

BOOKS BY GEORGE JOHNSTON

NON FICTION

Grey Gladiator   1941
Battle of the Seaways   1941
Australia at War   1942
New Guinea Diary   1943
Pacific Partner   1944
Skyscrapers in the Mist   1946
Journey Through Tomorrow   1947
The Australians   1966
Mosman Today   1967

FICTION

Death Takes Small Bites   1948
Moon at Perigee   1948
The Cyprian Woman   1955
The Darkness Outside   1959
Closer to the Sun   1960
The Far Road   1962
My Brother Jack   1964
The Far Face of the Moon   1964
Clean Straw for Nothing   1969
A Cartload of Clay   1971

UNDER THE PSEUDONYM OF SHANE MARTIN

Twelve Girls in the Garden   1957
The Saracen Shadow   1957
The Man Made of Tin   1958
The Myth is Murder   1959
A Wake for Mourning   1962

IN COLLABORATION WITH CHARMIAN CLIFT

High Valley   1949
The Big Chariot   1953
The Sponge Divers   1956

BOOKS BY CHARMIAN CLIFT

Mermaid Singing   1958
Peel Me a Lotus   1959
Walk to the Paradise Gardens   1960
Honour's Mimic   1964
Images in Aspic   1965
The World of Charmian Clift   1970

GEORGE JOHNSTON
AND
CHARMIAN CLIFT

Strong-man from Piraeus
and other stories

Chosen and Introduced by
GARRY KINNANE

PENGUIN BOOKS

Publication assisted by the Literature Board of the Australia
Council, the Federal Government's arts funding and advisory body

c.1

Penguin Books Australia Ltd,
487 Maroondah Highway, P.O. Box 257
Ringwood, Victoria, 3134, Australia
Penguin Books Ltd,
Harmondsworth, Middlesex, England
Penguin Books,
40 West 23rd Street, New York, N.Y. 10010, U.S.A.
Penguin Books Canada Limited,
2801 John Street, Markham, Ontario, Canada L3R 1B4
Penguin Books (N.Z.) Ltd,
182-190 Wairau Road, Auckland 10, New Zealand

First published 1984 by Thomas Nelson Australia
Published in Penguin, 1986

Offset from the Thomas Nelson edition
Made and printed in Australia by Dominion Press Hedges & Bell

CIP

Johnston, George, 1912-1970.
Strong-man from Piraeus and other stories.

ISBN 0 14 008798 2.

1. Short stories, Australian – 20th century. I. Clift,
Charmian, 1923-1969. II. Kinnane, Garry. III. Title.

A823'.0108

To Alice, Barbara and Lorraine
with gratitude

ACKNOWLEDGEMENTS

I wish to acknowledge the assistance of the staff of the Mitchell Library, Sydney, and the National Library, Canberra, whose co-operation was invaluable. I have also to thank Martin Johnston and the executors of the Johnston estate, as well as Kerryn Humphrey and Joanne Barron who typed the script.

'Astypalaian Knife' first appeared in *Cosmopolitan* (USA) in December 1955. 'Strong-man from Piraeus' first appeared in *Argosy* (UK) in October, 1956. 'Vale, Pollini!' first appeared in *Voices II* ed. Michael Radcliffe (Michael Joseph) 1965.

CONTENTS

CONTENTS

INTRODUCTION

Husband and wife teams are a rare thing, probably because most marriages cannot stand the strain of competition between partners. George Johnston and Charmian Clift, though each was an intense and strong-minded individual, managed through all the mixed fortunes their relationship inevitably underwent not only to stay together but also to deepen each other's commitment to the craft of writing. They read their work to each other, offered and accepted criticism, and were able to achieve enough harmony to produce three joint novels: testimony to their needs and respect for each other's creative ability. So – it seemed to me, on coming across a number of very readable unpublished stories while examining the Johnston estate papers, that in a posthumous anthology it would be fitting to keep the couple together.

The works in this volume represent a minor but important aspect of their writing. Known as novelists and journalists, they published very few short stories, and the stories in this collection not only show another side to their talents but extend our knowledge of them as writers – from their earliest days together in Sydney in the late 1940s until just before they left Greece for Australia in the 1960s. Moreover, the stories throw light on their expatriate existence during those years when it was impossible for Australian writers to subsist at home. How did Australians fare in the bigger cultural pond? What contact was there between Australia and Europe in the 1950s? These stories give the Johnstons' answer to such questions at a time when much was changing in their lives.

But this is to jump too far ahead, because the stories here take on more meaning when seen against a biographical background many readers will not be familiar with – despite the almost legendary status these two most romantic of Australian writers achieved in their lifetime. There was, indeed, something of the Scott-Fitzgerald and Zelda charisma about George and Charmian – except that Zelda wasn't a writer.

George Johnston's life is outlined in his best-selling novel *My Brother Jack*. He was born in 1912 into a Melbourne working-class family, and left school at fourteen to train as a lithographer. This kept him in work during the Depression. But he had always been interested in writing, and at the age of sixteen he began publishing articles on sailing ships in the Melbourne *Argus*. That was how his journalistic career began. When World War II broke out he was made Australia's first official war correspondent, and from then on his reputation blossomed spectacularly. Towards the end of the war, when his marriage to Elsie Taylor was failing, he met an astonishingly beautiful, green-eyed gunner in the AWAS: she was Charmian Clift, who apparently carried a copy of *Tristram Shandy* wherever she went.

Charmian's background was different from George's in one important respect: his childhood was totally suburban, hers was country. She was born in 1923 at Kiama on the south coast of New South Wales. Her father, Sid, was a Derbyshire man who had been to Cambridge and had come out to Australia to try his luck; he ended up as a mining engineer at the Kiama quarry. His bookshelves were well stocked with literature, and he especially loved Shakespeare – which is how Charmian came to be named after Cleopatra's attendant. Her mother was well-read and wrote poetry.

There had always been a serious interest in literature in the Clift household, but Charmian was by no means a blue-stocking. She and her brother and sister spent most of their childhood and youth roaming the rocks and lonely beaches round Kiama, and she refers to these times frequently in her writing. 'I vibrate in a storm like a tuning fork,' she wrote, 'and long for beaches, long, wave-lashed beaches, gulls, splinters, spars, dripping weed ... and a creek breaking its banks to make a playground for wild, wet children.'* This is true Charmian, with a passion, in the best Romantic tradition, for everything dramatic in nature.

It was her appetite for adventure that prompted her, along with her sister Margaret, to become an anti-aircraft trainee during the war. Charmian was posted to Melbourne, and there she met George Johnston. Her beauty, vitality, and interest in writing were more than George could resist; to her he was equally attractive – a dashing, famous reporter everyone called 'the golden boy'. And so their passionate adventure began. They married, moved to Sydney, began a family, and launched their joint writing careers.

In 1948 their first joint novel, *High Valley*, was acclaimed when it won the *Sydney Morning Herald* prize. It was inevitable that their desire for wider experience should take them abroad. Now on the editorial staff of the Sydney *Sun*, George was appointed to take charge of the London office, and in 1951 the Johnstons left for England. The plan was that George would continue his newspaper career while he wrote books part-time with Charmian. But the two roles proved incompatible, and in 1954 they abandoned London and journalism and went to the Greek islands to become full-time writers.

And in fact they managed happily enough, at least for the first four or five years. Living was relatively inexpensive in Greece, and some of their books began to do well, particularly in the United States. In 1956 they had a third child, Jason, and with the two older ones, Martin and Shane, attending the local school in Hydra, the brave experiment seemed to be working out. But things began to go wrong for them about 1958 onwards.

In the first place their fame was attracting hordes of drop-ins from all over the world, and these visitors made it increasingly difficult for the Johnstons to work: it was a great deal easier to drink, talk and waste energy. No doubt George and Charmian were partly to blame in failing to protect their privacy more

*'Winter Solstice', in *The World of Charmian Clift*, Ure Smith, 1970, p.60.

ruthlessly; but they were both kindly and sociable people and their hospitality was often exploited. Then George contracted tuberculosis, and the frustrating circumstances on Hydra made recovery there unlikely. So in 1964 the Johnstons came home to their own country, and within months of their return George's novel, *My Brother Jack*, was being praised everywhere as a work of lasting significance.

In the years after their return to Australia their writing matured and they received increasing recognition. George was turning *My Brother Jack* into a distinguished trilogy, and Charmian was commanding a massive following with her weekly column in the *Sydney Morning Herald*, which appeared in the Melbourne *Herald* as well. They were also writing film and television scripts.

Ironically, these years of consolidation in their work were also years of deep personal unhappiness. In 1969 readers everywhere were devastated to learn of Charmian's suicide; and then, a year later, never able to shake off tuberculosis, George also died. The pity of their premature deaths was that the best of their writing was only just beginning to come – as though to prove the old theory that suffering gives depth to an artist's work.

The stories in this volume may be said to come from a period when both writers were learning the craft of fiction. The first story is one of Charmian's very earliest, written about 1948 in Sydney. 'Even the Thrush Has Wings' is interesting for its lack of sentimentality in writing of a disabled child, a subject usually handled with heavy solemnity or else shunned altogether until recent years. Tina, the ten-year-old protagonist, has her own means of escape from a world of insensitive adults whose unconscious cruelty to the crippled child is as brutal as any violence.

Charmian's 'Three Old Men of Lerici' is one of several stories that came out of motoring tours in Europe between 1951 and 1954. Lerici is on the Bay of Spezia where the poet Shelley was drowned, and his presence haunts this story. The music of life itself comes like a revelation to the egotistical Ursula who has been behaving abominably to her devoted lover. At last she understands him.

'The Dying Day of Francis Bainsbridge' is a strange story in which George skilfully combines elements of modern mystery writing with the shape of a medieval morality tale. Was it some supernatural power that condemned Bainsbridge to death for his theft of the little Christ from the wayside shrine?

In 'Wild Emperor', Charmian's sensitive, poetic style is at its best in dealing with two very different people struggling to come to terms with their private fears, fears no less real for being unutterable. At times the suppressed violence between Doris and Josef has a Lawrentian vibrancy and decisiveness: 'There was no sound of their footfalls, and she felt the torment releasing in him. He was smooth and indistinct before her, his movement fluid and blended with the air – but she was a feverish glitter in the calm wood, diamond-hard in the diffuseness, and she stumbled through the gentians in a sudden agony of impatience.'

'Requiem Mass', written in 1952 or 1953, dramatises George's deep ambivalence about the kinds of cultured Europeans he was beginning to meet in London. The artist, Halliday, is a man of wide knowledge and considerable charm. As the narrator discovers, Halliday is also a collector, not only of *objets d'art*, but of people – such as his young actress wife Erica – whom he uses as background for his performance as artist and connoisseur. Mystery surrounds the reason why Halliday turns his house literally into a mausoleum.

Based on the Johnstons' arrival in Kalymnos in 1954, the first of the Greek stories, 'A Small Animus', is Charmian's light-hearted account of the difficult process of settling-in to a new house and a new life. It is a testimony to the unique warmth with which Greeks welcome foreigners into their midst.

In 'Sponge Boat' (1954 also), George deals dramatically with the conflicts among the crew, and shows an intimate knowledge of the subject that made the jointly written novel, *The Sponge Divers*, such a popular success. The atmosphere of tension and menace is splendidly maintained.

George's 'Astypalaian Knife' and 'Strong-man from Piraeus' are 1955 stories in a lighter vein showing the author's understanding of the customs that shape everyday life among the Greek islanders.

The final stories, both by George, are autobiographical evidence of why and how the Johnstons' Greek adventure went sour: George's illness and those intruding drop-ins on Hydra. 'The Verdict' was begun about 1958, soon after his tuberculosis was first diagnosed, and was finished some years later. It was knowing of his illness, more than anything else, that changed George's attitude to his writing. To him it was a death sentence and there is nothing like a death sentence to raise a person's consciousness of how much of his life and work he has wasted. George had spent far too much time and energy on hastily written pot-boiler novels. After he was told he had the illness he scarcely wrote another word that was not in deadly earnest – and how this new determination changed his writing! Suddenly there is a voice in his work – a clear, original voice with interesting and urgent things to say. This new spirit in his work produced the trilogy beginning with *My Brother Jack*.

In 'The Verdict' the painful events that triggered this change are dramatised, and the character of David Meredith, the figure who became Johnston's alter ego in his later fiction, appears for the first time. Meredith is shown here in the limbo of *waiting*, a situation that has become a 20th-century motif for spiritual alienation. As he wanders in Athens to fill in the day until his evening appointment with the doctor he looks back on his life and forward to the release the expected verdict will bring. But the verdict means he must battle on, and his reaction is one that has become a Johnston trademark: 'The smell of the crushed peppercorns was still on his fingers, and it brought back all his childhood, and he knew that nothing had been resolved and that he had to begin all over again. He felt so miserable he could have cried.'

Showing Meredith devastated, aching for the sanctuary of childhood, but doggedly courageous nevertheless, Johnston anticipates in this story with its spare, understated style the power and conviction of the trilogy he was to write.

The final story, 'Vale, Pollini!', written in the early 1960s but not published until 1965, shows Johnston at his most mature and engaging. The satirical humour of this story of an outrageous leg-pull hits back effectively at the name-dropping 'existentialists' who sponged so arrogantly on George and Charmian on Hydra, and makes one wish that George had written more often in this comic vein. How delightful it would be to know that this fiction really happened!

These stories are more openly informative about George and Charmian than anything else they wrote before 1964, filling out for us some of their imaginative life and actual experience at a time when their other writing revealed very little about the authors themselves. They had not yet discovered what kind of writers they were; yet all these stories are entertaining and evocative, with a pictorial quality that gives each scene vivid reality.

The stories will give readers an opportunity to compare the two styles: George, ever the reporter, relies on vivid descriptive passages and a clear, forceful development of events; Charmian, the romantic, has a more acute ear for the sound and colour of a sentence.

With their variety, range and liveliness, these stories will, I believe, give pleasure to thousands of Johnston/Clift devotees, and make a few converts as well.

Garry Kinnane

EVEN THE THRUSH
HAS WINGS

*

by *Charmian Clift*

Tina was ten when she learnt how to fly.

It was odd that the day began like any other. She wriggled out of bed at exactly half past six, being careful not to disturb Robert, still a small grey cocoon in his blankets.

She washed her face and hands at the kitchen sink – scrubbing very hard at her nose because old Daddy Hammond, who collected the garbage, had told her that scrubbing was the only way you could ever get the freckles off your nose. And he had laughed in a very jolly fashion so that his face creased up round and red and juicy-looking as a tomato, and he had chucked her under the chin with a juicy red hand that smelt of stale fish and bananas and potato peelings.

'Never mind then, my pretty,' he had told her. 'It's a little speckled thrush you are – there's nothing I like better than a little speckled thrush.'

Tina had felt uncomfortable, because, although she knew he was trying to be nice, she didn't much like being called a little speckled thrush. Still, there might have been something in what he'd said about the scrubbing – so Tina scrubbed.

And after she had scrubbed she went back to the bedroom and buttoned her skinny little body into her dark-blue everyday dress and tied a clean pinny over it, and strained her wet hair back into skimpy pigtails.

She looked at her nose very carefully in the mirror. There was only a slice of mirror left. Most of it was black where the silver had gone. The bottom part was just like a dragon, but the top part, where Tina had once scratched with a pin to make a St George out of a shapeless blob, didn't look like anything except a shapeless blob bigger than the old one. She cocked her head sideways, but the freckles were still there, like little flecks of melted butter all running into each other. Tina sighed – but very softly, because of little Robert – and went out to the kitchen to help Mum with the breakfast.

Mum was a big woman, but big in a soggy sort of way, so that Tina always felt that if she pushed her finger into one of those soft, white curls of flesh the dent would take a long time to come out. Mum's face was soft and soggy, too, like a crushed pansy. It always wore an expression of forbearance, although Mum didn't often speak the way her face looked. But Tina could always read the forbearing expression without the need of words, and so she always tried very hard to be useful about the house, and she hoped that one day Mum's face would lose the look for a little while.

Tina took the wooden ladle and stirred diligently at the porridge squelching and sucking in the big black saucepan.

'Oh, Tina dear,' Mum sighed on a great exhaling note. 'I wish you wouldn't keep getting under my feet. There's so much to do and I really haven't time. Really . . . there's a *good* girl.'

Tina swallowed and left the porridge and began to sweep the floor, being very careful to get all the crumbs out of the cracks in the lino. You could do it if you used the edge of the broom. And then Dad came from the bedroom in a terrific hurry and tripped on the broom.

Dad was angry when he picked himself up, and he pulled Tina to her feet with an unnecessary jerk, and Mum sighed and said: 'Oh, Tina, really! *Do* go outside until breakfast's ready . . . there's a good girl. There's so much to do. . . . ' And her eyes were moist with forbearance.

Tina took the broom with her and she swept the concrete steps. Her angular little face was peaked in concentration. She picked the dead leaves off the passionfruit vine until Mum called her in to breakfast.

'Tina, now do try to hurry ... there's a good girl. You know it takes you a long time to walk to school and you don't want to be late again.'

But school had gone in by the time Tina slid clumsily to her seat, painfully conscious of the cessation of Miss Appleby's precise voice and the crease of irritation between Miss Appleby's precise spectacles. And Miss Appleby sighed on a note of forbearance strongly reminiscent of Mum, and murmured with a rather wearied kindliness: 'All right, Tina ... but won't you *please* try to start off from home a little earlier in future?'

The day pulled at every ink-smelling hour, and it was full of historical dates and elementary algebra and the precise punctuation of Miss Appleby's voice and Willie Morris throwing paper darts with pen-nib points at the cracked plaster roof until Miss Appleby stood him in the corner because she didn't believe in caning her pupils.

Tina concentrated very hard on those mysterious, muddling symbols of x and y and a multiplied by b in brackets, and Miss Appleby looked quite pleased and put a purple star in her exercise book. Tina felt better after that. Perhaps if she really studied hard she'd get to be a brilliant scholar and a useful citizen and Mum and Dad would be terribly proud of her and Mum's face wouldn't look crumpled any more.

Then after the lunch recess Miss Appleby jerked stiffly down the room and climbed on to the dais and rapped the desk sharply with the long wooden ruler. Her precise, lemon-colour face was bright with portent.

'Now, young people,' she chirped crisply (Miss Appleby never called her pupils 'children'), 'I have a pleasant surprise for you. The committee of the Flower Festival has written to ask the

3

school to take part – and I have decided that you young people shall give a display of folk dancing.' Miss Appleby was very keen about folk dancing. She always said that even if she was merely a country girl herself teaching in a country school she could, at least, pride herself on her modern ideas about education.

'Now,' she continued, 'this afternoon I shall pick two teams – a team from the boys and a team from the girls – and when I have picked the teams we shall devote the remainder of the afternoon to practice.'

She glowed on the dais like a creased yellow lantern, and as the whispers began to buzz up from the desks she rapped again with the ruler.

'Now, now, young people, there is still one more thing. The teams will, of course, be dressed in appropriate costume. But it is you young people who are to give the display and I feel that *you* should choose the colour scheme. *I* think that pink and blue would be very appropriate, but I intend to leave the decision with you. Now then?'

Tina's heart whirred and jumped like a broken alarm clock. She could see the dancers weaving a pattern on the grass under the bright flame of the coral-trees, and the parents watching proudly, and all the committee nodding their heads and beaming. She put up one bony little hand.

'Please, Miss Appleby – wouldn't red and white be nice? The same red as the coral-trees?'

Miss Appleby's face went a slightly deeper yellow, and her spectacles spun light as she threw up her hands and broke into tinkling chirps of laughter.

'Oh, Tina dear – *really*! *Red* and *white*? For folk dancing?'

And the rest of the class giggled, and then Angela Watts tossed her long yellow curls and snickered as she put up her hand.

'Please, Miss Appleby. I think pink and blue would be *lovely*!'

Miss Appleby shone. 'Why, there now! What a charming suggestion. Young people! Angela has suggested pink and blue for the costume, and I think you will agree that nothing could be more appropriate. Thank you, Angela. And now for the teams.'

Tina sat very still and watched the curds of sunlight flecking across the desk and tried to look as though it didn't matter when Miss Appleby's voice hovered and pounced on names that sent little spurts of delight popping up all around her. Once she looked up and met Miss Appleby's eyes and Miss Appleby's eyes flickered away hurriedly and she stumbled on the next name. She knew that Miss Appleby was embarrassed and angry with her because she, Tina, had caused the embarrassment. The knowledge made Tina curl up inside, because she didn't want to be an embarrassment to anybody.

She wondered, wistfully, if she ever would stop being an embarrassment to grown-ups, and then she realised that Miss Appleby's voice had clicked off without calling Angela Watts's name, and Angela was squirming and tossing her curls as if she didn't care.

'And now,' Miss Appleby's voice clicked on again, 'we must of course have a little queen of the dance who will have nothing to do but lead the dancers in and then . . . ha, ha . . . queen it over them.'

Tina's heart lurched. Please, she whispered inside herself, please, please, please, *please*! Just this once let me have something special. Let Miss Appleby pick me for queen. Oh, please. And I'll never ask for anything special again. Just this once. Let me have a blue dress and a crown and lead the dancers in and make Mum proud of me. Please!

And something of that inward whisper must have shone through her eager, peaked face, because Miss Appleby's hovering gaze caught on Tina's pleading eyes and for an endless moment rested there.

Please, Tina whispered inside, *please*.

You could almost see Miss Appleby's eyes relaying to Miss Appleby's brain the total effect of a skinny, undersized body, a

5

thin and patient face splotched with freckles, two enormous wistful eyes, and a couple of skimpy pigtails of very ordinary and very uninteresting mouse-brown.

Miss Appleby's eyes became unstuck from Tina's and were suddenly intent on the tip of the ruler. A slow flush crept under the yellow of Miss Appleby's cheeks.

Then she looked up and spoke very crisply: 'I think Angela will make a very pretty queen and be a credit to us all.'

'Tina, haven't you any homework to do?' Mum asked after tea. 'It isn't good for you just to *sit around*. Now, there's a good girl....'

Tina looked up at Mum, and Mum seemed soft and soggy and comfortable and her eyes were moist and puzzled, and suddenly Tina was nuzzling into the big white bosom, choking out the tale of the folk dancing, and Miss Appleby, and how she wanted to be the queen in a blue dress and a crown.

The soggy hands fluttered helplessly. 'Oh, Tina dear, really... I wish you weren't so *sensitive*. It makes everything so difficult.'

'Chin up, lass!' Dad bellowed with awkward cheerfulness. 'Can't have self-pity, you know! And your mother and I have both had a hard day. Now run along to bed, and stop worrying about things that don't matter. Chin up, now!'

The bedroom was cool and quiet and dark when Tina slid noiselessly between the sheets. Green shadows moved quietly across the ceiling, gliding and splodgy, like sunlight on the bed of the creek; the everyday furnishings wavered, half-sensed, in a new and dusky mystery. Robert snuffled in his sleep. Outside, the big blue street lamp seemed to hang unsupported in the dark frame of the window, and a million little winged things went clicketing round the cool blue sphere in a frenzy of whirring flight. The muslin curtains stirred against the wall.

Tina lay quietly, without movement, without tears, and

watched the shimmering dance that looped a swirl of aloof radi-
ance around the street light. She wanted to cry. But if she cried
she might wake Robert – and, anyway, Dad was right. Self-
pity wasn't much use. But then what WAS any use? She
wouldn't care so much about dancing and things like that if she
were pretty like Angela Watts or clever at school or if Mum
would say just once that she was a help around the house. Oh,
Tina whispered, I wish I was one of those little insects with lovely
coloured wings flying round and round in beautiful blue light.
Flying so lightly, drifting and soaring in the frame of the window.
It looked so easy: Even Tina might almost stretch out her arms
and dart upwards and turn and pause and float into that cool blue
light.

'Oooo-ooh!' Tina breathed, finding herself suspended, arms
outstretched, three feet above the bed – and immediately she
fell back again with a little muffled thump.

She touched the bedclothes, tentatively, and the round knob
on the bedpost, and cautiously fluttered her fingers over her own
face, and stretched over to peer intently into Robert's cot.
Warmth and wonder and an overpowering happiness seeped
along her skinny body and tingled in her fingertips. She stretched
her arms again and sucked in a very deep breath.

There! It happened again! She was floating above the bed,
rocking – a little awkwardly it was true – but she couldn't
quite get her balance while she was still on her back. She gave her
body a cautious twist and rolled over and corrected her balance
with a jiggling movement of legs and arms.

She felt strange and light and cool, as if she had breathed in
some of the thin blue mist that clung to the street lamp and was
supported by it. It didn't really seem odd that she should be
rocking in the air above her bed. It seemed a familiar thing that
she had done many times before and had only just remembered.
And now all she had to do was to give her arms a tiny wiggle

and push with bent knees, and she would soar out through the window, out into the warm, insect-heavy night . . . like that!

Tina's nose and the window-frame connected with an unpleasant thwack and her legs became entangled in her nightgown as she crashed. There was a blinding pain inside her head, but she was able to crawl back into bed before the room span into darkness.

'Tina, what *have* you done to your nose? Really, child, I have so much to worry about . . . you *must* be more careful.'

But Tina was stirring the porridge happily, and she murmured something about falling out of bed and hitting the bedpost, and then she skipped back to her bedroom to look in the slice of mirror.

And this morning she did not really see the freckles or the skimpy pigtails or St George and the Dragon — she saw only the wide, unlovely bruise, and her heart sang at its loveliness. It was all true — and it was better than dancing or being a brilliant scholar or anything — or anything at all. She had flown! And if she had flown once then she could fly again. Tonight she could fly — *every* night! Out of the window and away over the fields and the farms and up into the wide bright sky.

'Tina!' Mum was calling plaintively. 'Hurry up now . . . there's a *good* girl. You'll be late again.'

'Coming, Mum dear!' Tina called, and all her happiness chirrupped in her thin little voice. She planted a small, radiant kiss on Mum's crumpled cheek as she grabbed her satchel and hurried to the gate.

'Well!' Mum murmured. 'What on earth's got into the child?' She smiled in a faint perplexity as she watched the little bobbing figure that hurried down the road.

And then it occurred to her that the bump on the head might have done something the doctors hadn't been able to do. She shrugged away the possibility. Still, funnier things had happened. Certainly Tina was walking straighter on that withered, crippled leg than she could ever remember before.

THREE OLD MEN OF LERICI

*

by Charmian Clift

The day, after all, had remained hot. It was nearly evening when the car flung itself over the hill – Freiburg's thumb was jammed irritably on the horn: he had had enough of damned lunatic Italian motorists for one day – and under the deepening sky, still strewn with those big lazy whoofs of cloud that had, after all, come to nothing, they hurtled down on Lerici.

'Wake up, Ursula! We've arrived!' Freiburg felt more cheerful suddenly. He liked arrivals.

Down they swooped, down through the villas and the red and purple vines, and Ursula, who had been slumped apathetic against the sticky plastic upholstery for the last hour – eyes closed behind her dark glasses in a stupor of heat and misery – straightened her back and reared her long neck questioningly. Freiburg took a corner with tremendous dash, leaning with the car, rejoicing childishly in its power, showing off a bit for the benefit of the basking villas. He had a queerly ecstatic vision of the car leaping from one of the hilltops and sailing on through the evening, right over Lerici and into the Gulf of Spezia. There it was, spinning round beneath them, a great breadth of wrinkled peacock silk, flecked all over with tiny moving scraps of white and crimson and blue, and with white towns edging it.

Ursula took off her glasses and peered down, blinking. It was too bright! Too agonisingly bright! It hurt her eyes to look at it. Three squashy little yellow stars leapt on the dusty windscreen in front of her. Really, she ought not to have discouraged him from buying one of those plastic deflector things, even at the risk of pandering to his tendencies towards vulgarity. But those insects! She picked another tiny stunned body off her crumpled skirt and began rummaging in the big Florentine straw bag for comb and mirror. The wind-scoops had been open all day, and the burning blasts of air had whipped her hair into a dry, frizzy tangle, and caked her make-up into a gritty mask that pulled her muscles down and down. Oh why, why had she let Pierre perm her hair? It was too light, too fine. And why in heaven's name did she go on making up her face every morning? She knew well enough what these long hot days in the car did to it. She ought to just scrub well and slap some astringent on, and a touch of lipstick. Then she would still look fresh at the end of the day instead of . . . instead of . . . oh, damn this clear, harsh Italian light! *You don't dare any more*, the face in the mirror said sullenly, and the strained, dust-rimmed eyes welled with tired tears.

Lerici shimmered and wavered, and Freiburg eased his foot off the accelerator as it rushed up to meet them. They crawled in through a voluble, admiring populace and nosed along beside the sea, Freiburg's thumb still on the musical horn.

'Oh, my God!' Ursula breathed shakily. 'The Shelley Restaurant!' A *plage*! A casino! It was a *resort*!

'Look, darling,' Freiburg said, darting a quick, concerned glance at her, 'I'll run up a bit and turn and work back to that market place. Looks like the old town there.'

It was Ursula who negotiated for their room, rocking backwards and forwards on her heels between the dusty potted shrubs, sick with tiredness. Like a marionette the *padrone* bowed, twirled, flicked his fingers, darted an oblique bright glance, hopped back a pace or two, considered Ursula, rocking rocking, and behind her the dusty silver-grey car with the gleaming club badges and the radio aerial, and Freiburg, who couldn't get the hang of languages, pretending to adjust the windscreen wipers, vaguely ashamed that Ursula always had to do this sort of thing.

Chattering groups detached themselves from the swarms under the market awnings and came to stare, to discuss, to conjecture. Children gathered, grouped about the car like ragged bunches of flowers. Beyond a stone parapet the clear waters of the bay slapped and sighed against gay little boats: 'Only two fifty *lire*, mister' . . . a blue-jerseyed boy grinned hopefully . . . 'Right around the bay . . . .'

Freiburg tried a smile at the children. '*Bella*, eh?' he said, patting the car.

'All right,' Ursula said shortly, returning. 'We can't have a private bath. They're full up, or pretty well.'

'Garage?' Freiburg asked, quite humble.

'Damn!' She clenched her fists with exasperation. Really! Why, in heaven's name? She had to think of everything. Everything . . . while he stood around showing off to a pack of kids she was expected to . . . . It was too much!

The *padrone* watched from the cavernous doorway, showing all his teeth, and past him a thin dark sliver of a boy, wrapped all about in a snowy apron that was crossed over his narrow buttocks, cleaved through the sunlight in two leaps and stood beside them, smiling extravagantly.

'Give him the bags,' Ursula said wearily, closing her eyes against the brutal light and all the curious dark glances fixed upon her. 'I'll ask about the garage later.'

Freiburg handed out two pigskin cases, and after a moment's deliberation he took both cameras as well, and the leather briefcase that contained their passports, and the roadmaps and pamphlets. It was a bit late for photography today perhaps, but Ursula might feel better after a wash and brush-up, and the market would compose quite well, with that queer, crumbly little clock-tower in the background. Need a filter, though, to get the best out of it; and then there was the question of the light. He rummaged for the leather accessory bag and stowed it in the briefcase, rather furtively. Well, it wasn't safe to leave things like that in cars, anyway. He'd known fellows who'd had cameras lifted while they were having lunch.

'Americano?' a voice piped winningly, and the children broke and clustered around him, grinning and holding out their little brown claws. 'Shewing gum? Cigaret?'

'My *God*!' Ursula said, and stalked off into the hotel behind the boy with the bags. Horribly, right in the centre of her shoulder-blades, she could feel the dispassionate scrutiny of the still group of men clustered in the open doorway pasted all round with Communist posters. The men were black and unmoving, like part of the posters, printed against the red lettering, watching her.

Freiburg looked after her uneasily. But then a bell clanged surprisingly from the weed-grown clock-tower, and clanged again, swinging its big grey mouth so heavily away that it seemed as if the tower, already tilting dangerously, must inevitably collapse into a mound of old tired dust. The clock showed six forty-five. Freiburg stared at it, his jaw fallen in surprise, but the bell was still, the last of its two single echoes hanging metallically in the high excited buzz of the market. Freiburg laughed. Crazy! Wonderfully crazy!

'Here!' He called suddenly to the children, and held out a handful of small coins. Funny little beggars . . . eyes like pansies! Prettiest kids in the world!

Ursula, flinging up the window of their room, looked down to see Freiburg, hung ridiculously with his cameras, smiling down with a queer, tender sort of joy at a score of ragged children who clamoured around him screeching. She turned back into the cool dark room, shaking.

At the head of one white bed the boy glimmered like a taper, erect above the pigskin bags, waiting expectantly.

'You may go,' she said curtly. 'The signor,' she added, puckering her eyes to see him in the darkness, and speaking very slowly to make sure he understood, 'the signor will see to your tip, and the registration.'

Let him damn well do it himself for once. That long curious scrutiny of the passports, the speculative glance from her to Freiburg, Freiburg hovering behind her, humming carelessly, oblivious – how many times had she writhed? 'But why do you *care*, darling girl?' he would say. '*They* don't. They adore it, don't you see?' Well, if he didn't mind let him muddle through it himself for a change.

But when the boy had gone she ran to the door of the room and called after him down the long cool corridor:

'And if you would show the signor where to put his car?'

The boy turned at the stair-well and looked back at her, ears pricked like a faun's.

'The signor worries,' Ursula called softly, as if an explanation were necessary. 'It is a valuable car.'

But she was tired, tired. Weary to the bone. Somehow the Shelley Restaurant had been just too much. *Lines Written in the Bay of Lerici*. Was there nowhere in all the world beyond the reach of vulgarity and commercialism any longer? In some queer way she had high hopes of Lerici – as though the name and its associations could somehow break down the barriers of irritability and misunderstanding that had been building up between them ever since they had set out – as though, even now, it might be possible to . . . .

She kicked off her shoes viciously – those fine flat Venetian shoes, soft and smooth as gloves, extravagantly simple. She had winced translating the price to him. If only, afterwards, he had not so obviously yearned for a gondola, forcing her to suggest it: all the ancient, remote magic of Venice spoilt, ruined utterly, irretrievably, by that horrible touristy ride, and the gondolier – hard, crafty, oh so contemptuous! – waiting until they slid by the crowded Rialto steps to suddenly throw back his Latin-lover head and pour out a ridiculous cascade of song. And Freiburg smiling at her so tenderly, so happily, quite unable to see how humiliating it was.

Stealthily she paddled over the worn tiles – arching her feet against the wonderful coolness. The huge, gilt-framed mirror caught her, and she looked at herself for a while, sullenly, with no sense of recognition. *I shouldn't have come with him.* She turned away from the tired caricature of herself and began unpacking. Everything rumpled, everything travel-stained. She wanted to cry. Hesitantly she unfolded the narrow linen trousers and the white poplin shirt he had bought for her in Rome. She had been saving them – her last reserve of elegance. The shirt would never survive more than two wearings. She stood by the case, smoothing them over and over. *I'm too old*, she thought with sudden bleak honesty, *for this sort of thing*.

And yet the prospect had been so charming. Freiburg lolling at her feet in front of the blazing February fire, and the rubbed velvet curtains drawn against the Chelsea mist. Pouring tea from the lovely Rockingham pot she had picked up for a song in the Portobello Road, and the firelight dancing on the glowing surfaces of her few perfect pieces of furniture, and the red and blues and golds of her books glinting like a very old tapestry spread against the wall. Freiburg's chestnut eyes – *like a very intelligent fox terrier's*, she used to think, with tender amusement – eager and ardent, yet humble, and his sensitive freckled hand stroking her instep while her voice murmured on wistfully, bringing the sunshine of Italy into the room, and the splendour of the Renaissance, San Gimignano's towers, the flag-dancers of Siena, the taste of sunwarmed grapes. She could hear herself sighing, and see the half-rueful smile curving her mouth.

'Oh, damn!' she said loudly to the jaded creature sulking in the mirror; and laid out the linen pants, the poplin shirt.

When Freiburg came, sidling cautiously into the room, his eyes wary but his face on the brink of a beam of sheer happiness, she had finished with her make-up case and was brushing a touch of brilliantine into her hair to soften the curls.

'Darling!' He moved towards her. 'Turn around. You look like George Sand! Lovely! Absolutely lovely! No wonder the old boy downstairs slapped me on the back.'

Outside a bell tolled, once, and then a series of small bells broke in with an unrelated clamour.

'That clock!' Freiburg laughed. 'That crazy, wonderful clock!' He pushed his head and shoulders through the window. 'Come and see, darling,' he called. 'The market's packing up. And there's an old woman with a basket scaling fish on the sea wall. And a ferryboat going out – bursting at the seams with trippers.'

Broken threads of song drifted across the bay from the gaudy pleasure boat. In the dusky golden light that filled the market place the crowds swirled and eddied, and above them the scarlet and blue and yellow awnings swayed and collapsed and were borne away wrapped tight about their poles. A frieze of men and women carrying on their heads trays of shoes and clothing moved in stately procession around the base of the clock-tower. The old Mother Carey on the sea wall plunged and dipped and rose again in the blinking red eye of the sun, dappled all over with silver, and in her wicker creel the heaped fish glittered like jewels.

Ursula put down her brush, and hung two tiny silver hoops in her ears. In the mirror George Sand watched her aloofly, and then smiled, mollified.

She curled up gracefully on the window-ledge beside Freiburg and rubbed her pointed chin into his shoulder. How nice he smelt, always, and how absurdly young was that soft drake's tail of chestnut hair on the brown nape of his neck.

'If you'll suspend your enchantment for long enough to wash

16

that grubby face of yours,' she said, 'you can take me for a little walk up to the *castello* before dinner.'

'Of course,' Ursula continued, 'the plain fact is Shelley was too highly original for his contemporaries. You must remember that. Pure intellect made them uncomfortable. And then practising idealism as well as preaching it. I suppose if he had stayed at home and gone mad with silly little Harriet and that awful harpy Eliza they would have found it easier to forgive him. Don't you think?'

Freiburg nodded acquiescence and smiled sidelong at the women peeling vegetables in the dark, narrow doorways. They were like pigeons, he thought: plump and soft and quiet except for the alert movements of their smooth heads as they called to each other. The steep, dirty little canyons seemed to be filled with a liquid murmuring that paused as they passed, and welled up again behind them.

'. . . to avoid actuality,' Ursula concluded, and pulled his sleeve lightly to emphasise her point. Freiburg turned his warm, credulous face to her and captured her hand in his. He was so happy he could . . . he didn't care who was looking . . . .

'Oh, do look at the fishwives,' Ursula said. 'I'll swear they've been sitting on those same doorsteps since Shelley walked past. Queer, isn't it, how insensitive the human animal can be? How anyone could loll there in that appalling stench! Shall we go back and ask *them* what they thought of Mary Godwin?'

Freiburg earnestly turned Mary Godwin over in his mind, trying to see her, but all that emerged was a picture of Ursula's thin clever face pointed disdainfully over some sort of rich trailing dress, and all the fishwives bobbing curtsies. He felt vaguely ashamed of his own romanticism of a moment before. *Pigeons*!

Above them the warm castle walls lifted against the dark sky. They climbed the last flight of slippery steps out of the old town, panting a little, Ursula's hand still caught tight in his.

'Pitched betwixt heaven and the *plage*,' Ursula said. 'At least they haven't turned it into a casino.'

Below them the purpling bay was brushed with gold. Two black-rigged fishing boats slid like shadows into the crowded anchorage, and a ferryboat left the wharf, pricked all over with pale lights, irritably spitting steam. The daytime trippers were leaving, the fishermen coming home. Freiburg, watching the lights moving across the water, was filled with a soft, beautiful melancholy. Ursula prowled about with her slow, graceful stride, pleasantly conscious of her own angular black and white elegance moving in the dusk. There was, she thought, something quite sublime about heights. If only one need never descend to the neon lights! A breeze tugged her hair, gently, and Freiburg's arm stole about her shoulders and turned her to him. *Why*, she thought, in sudden surprised happiness, *this is* . . . .

A plump red-headed girl with a flowered seersucker skirt sticking damply to her wet bathing costume heaved over the railings and disappeared around the castle wall.

'Veronica! Ron-n-n-ie!' They could hear her high voice wailing. 'Chuck us a towel, do! I'll drip through the hall otherwise!'

'Good heavens!' Ursula said, 'What do you suppose . . . ?'

Two very hefty young men wearing leather shorts and boots strode across the courtyard, and with a cursory glance at Freiburg and Ursula marched off down the steps into the old town, arguing as they went. Their thick German voices rumbled all the way down the narrow street.

'Of *course*!' Freiburg said. 'The castello must be a youth hostel. Lucky young beggars! . . . What's the matter, darling? Ursula?' But Ursula was striding off down the steps, and when he caught her she refused his arm and thrust her hands into the pockets of her pants, dragging the seams. They returned to the hotel in silence, walled about by their separate miseries.

In front of the hotel, behind the dusty potted shrubs, twelve tables had been pushed together, and the white-aproned boy flickered around them like a moth, touching bowls of fruit, wicker-cradled bottles of Chianti, carafes of rough wine, shallow baskets heaped with bread. The *padrone* appeared, twirling, bowing. *The signor and the signora had had a pleasant walk? The castello was fine, was it not? And the view? Their table? Quite ready . . . if the signor and signora would follow him to the dining-room.*

'We prefer to dine outside,' Ursula said coldly.

He was desolated. On any other night . . . but as the signor and signora saw — all the outside tables . . . tonight there was to be a celebration, a reunion . . . .

'What is he saying?' Freiburg asked.

Ursula explained with tight control. The *padrone* smiled and smiled, and the white-aproned boy regarded them softly with his velvet eyes.

'Tell him we'll dine somewhere else, then,' Freiburg said gently.

'Tell him yourself!' Ursula grimaced, and she fixed Freiburg with a wide cold stare that might at any moment be blurred with tears. 'Tell him anything you damn well please! *I* intend to have a tray sent up.' And halfway up the stairs she turned and looked down on him, as he stood smiling foolishly and apologetically at the *padrone*, 'Why don't you go and eat at the Shelley?' she called shakily. 'I'm sure you'd love it.'

She had been standing at the darkened window for a long time. She didn't know how long. She never wore a watch; the thin threadlike pointers frightened her somehow, spinning so fast. Like wearing one's death on one's wrist.

In the square the evening promenade had thinned out to a few gossiping fishermen, loath to relinquish the warm night, and two small boys, who, in spite of repeated shooing from the *padrone*, continued to loiter, watching the party assemble self-consciously around the tables beneath her window. In the lighted window of the Communist office a man in shirt sleeves sat hunched over a typewriter, picking out the letters with two fingers.

The bell on the ludicrous tower tolled again, maddeningly, swinging its great open mouth up to the stars, and all the little bells set up an insane clamour. A jazzy orange moon shot up into the sky and hung among the jangling echoes, lighting the square like a Chinese lantern. The clock on the tower had stopped at nine minutes past seven.

The chubby carafes moved across the white cloth below. White napkins fluttered and opened their folds over anonymous, dark-suited knees. The glass and the silver winked on the whiteness with an intolerable glitter; the mountains of fruit exploded with colour. Behind a great platter of scampi the *padrone*'s smile stretched into a wide, winking arc, tilted up to her window. The little bells began to peal again, with irritable haste.

Ursula moved back from the window slyly, one foot behind the other, letting the curtain fall from her fingers fold by fold. The room leapt back to bright normality, and she stood by the light switch, blinking uneasily at her nightclothes laid out on the high white bed that seemed so isolated on the vast checkerboard of tiles. The light from the naked bulb pendant among shadowy cupids was clear and harsh. A clinical light. Alone in the bare bright room she felt somehow . . . *exposed*.

The thing was, of course, that she must not allow herself to become so tired in future. Everything got out of proportion. She would tell Freiburg in the morning – very gently, of course – that she simply could not go on at this pace. 'It isn't fair, my dear,' she would point out, 'to either of us.'

With an air of decision she unfolded her nightgown and walked briskly across the room to the window. Very firmly she closed the shutters.

But in bed in the dark the sheets were cold and slippery. She slid her toes up and down. A roughened piece of skin caught and rasped against the sheet and she twisted in sudden exasperation. Something *else* to be attended to tomorrow. Her feet were always as smooth and well-tended as her hands. Details like that were so important. You couldn't let up on all the little things, and lately there hadn't been time. How many dusty sightseeing miles had she tramped in the past weeks? No, she would have to be firm with Freiburg in the morning.

He *must* have had dinner by this time. Probably he was down by the water somewhere, mooning about. Lonely, humiliated . . . .

A great shout of laughter buffetted the shutters. The big bell began to toll again, and all the little ones, utterly demented with the warm air and the full-blown moon.

With her eyes closed she tried to relax from the forehead down as she had been taught by Dr Heinrich. Frown and then relax the muscles; the frown smooths out and the muscles become limp. Next the eyes. Roll the eyeballs downwards as if you were looking at an imaginary black spot on your toes. A rough piece of skin there. And her eyes felt horribly puffy. She *must* get to sleep before Freiburg returned. Those swollen throbbing eyes put her at such a disadvantage. He would think her hideous. *Old*. No. No. He adored her. Worshipped her. With my body I thee worship . . . . Tension is muscular contraction . . . relaxation is muscular limpness . . . black skin on her toes . . . .

Suppose he was not mooning. Suppose he had picked up a girl, a soft Italian girl with great shivery breasts and a milky bloom to her skin, and was worshipping her with his body in the moonlight. Oh, it wasn't fair! It wasn't fair! He'd have been nothing without her guidance and encouragement. Nothing! She had taught him everything he knew of sensitivity, appreciation, all the finer things. She tossed, desperately, and a tear trickled down the side of her nose.

Clench your teeth together . . . let go. Feel the weight of your lower jaw as it sags. Sags. Sagging jaw. No. No. He was sulking. That was it. Small boy sulking. Rather sweet. Exasperating, of course, but forgivable. I can't sleep . . . *I can't sleep* . . . the noise . . . those damned bells . . . *I can't sleep* . . . .

Yet she did sleep, for when she first heard the pipe it was very thin and far away, and so high it was almost beyond the threshold of sound. There was nothing else, neither laughter nor bells, but after a time a faint thrumming rose and fell behind the reed, like the beating of innumerable tiny wings over a summer pond. Ah, don't! Ursula cried silently, don't hurt me like that. But the little wings were beating in her head, and the pipe pierced her like sunlight. But it's too bright, too agonisingly bright, she protested. It hurts me terribly! And her eyes were so swollen, too. It wasn't fair.

She awoke stumbling across the room to the shutters to put it out. To fling the shutters wide and put it out.

'Oh, my God!' she thought hysterically, leaning against the window and looking down into the square. 'There's a variety turn as well!'

The square was white with moonlight and wild with music. She looked down on broken bread and spilt wine and scraps of food congealing on oily plates and ashtrays spilling butts over the soiled tablecloth; and now all the diners were leaning forward, quite still, each dark head immobilised at the very moment of attention, turned towards a lively triangle at the head of the table. There, ludicrous in their age and poverty, three very old men in round-crowned hats and shabby coats bent bobbing shoulders over pipe and strings, jigging out a measure to their own music. Their thin old legs bent, fragile and brittle-looking as twigs beneath their flapping rags, shuffling out a spritely parody of youth, and as they shuffled they tilted their heads, each in a listening attitude, as if they were translating some secret thing they heard in the night.

Shuffle to the right, shuffle to the left . . . the strings thrummed and the pipe rose and lingered and fell and rose again effortlessly . . . a reedy sound, bubbling, pithy, a reed still wet with the river . . . the mouth curved over it wide, flat, fleshy, and the eyes above the mouth flat too, hooded, lashless, with a thick fold of skin at the outer corners.

But she couldn't *see* their faces! It would not be so awful if she could see the old men's faces! Lewd old men, jigging obscenely to their indecent music! It hurt — it hurt so terribly! She wanted to summon up a picture of her glowing books, her rubbed velvet curtains, her Rockingham pot, the cool conversations among the thin old china teacups. Her barriers. But the unseen face intervened, wide, flat, curving, white as the moon, tender over the reed, and now the wet bubbling sound of the reed was everywhere in the night: it ran along the cobbles, gushed from the clock-tower, it lapped with the waves against the seawall, it welled from the tiles under Ursula's feet. The old men whirled among the potted shrubs, grotesque in their age and stiffness, blown rags in a wild wind of their own making. Ursula felt — she ought to feel — outraged. It seemed an outrageous thing was happening to her. As if . . . *why*, she thought, groping feverishly on the outskirts of memory, *I know . . . .*

But just as her mind stumbled in surprised recognition the strings twangled into silence and the last high gurgling note of the pipe floated out over the sea and was gone. And now the still figures around the table were moving, raising their hands, clapping, the old men were bowing stiffly, their knees bent outwards. The diners leaned towards each other, shouting ribaldries. The old men accepted wine and, drinking it, huddled together among the shrubs, as if for reassurance. A fat Italian lurched to his feet and began making a speech. The top buttons of his trousers were undone and there were stains on his shirt front. It was over.

In the window Ursula shivered, as though the impersonal coldness of the moon had seeped through to her bones, and stumbled back to the high white bed. She was cold now, stretched out empty and desolate in the sterile moonlight, colder than she had ever been. She would always be cold now. Because Freiburg would not come back. She thought of him with the warm girl on the sand, and she knew that his eyes would hold no wariness, and his forehead would no longer be puckered with vague puzzled shame. He would not even have heard the extraordinary music.

But then, she thought, with an old familiar envy stirring tiredly, *Freiburg hears it all the time.*

He heard it all the time. But that was *it*, of course! That was this thing about Freiburg. That was what she had resented in him all this time – and envied – calling it vulgarity. She was always distracted by the discordant notes, but Freiburg was simple and humble enough to hear them as part of the pattern. And it seemed suddenly to her that if one could only hear it the pipe played always – if one knew how to listen, as Freiburg did. Perhaps, after all, there was nothing grotesque or impious in the raucous shouts of drunken laughter that had succeeded the old men's music. The grotesqueries were part of it. The laughter went on fluting up and up . . . one peal of laughter and another chasing it . . . and another . . . and the bells mixed up in the laughter . . . or was it the pipe again? All the bells pealing with laughter at the ironical pipe . . . yes, it *was* the pipe, leading them on with the most absurd and delirious comments . . . ever higher, ever clearer . . . up and up and up . . . . The bells all crashed together with discordant chimes – three – and were quiet.

When she awoke again the music was fading. The strings thrummed and the reed danced on three notes, lightly, lightly sadly fading. The room was moon-grey and Freiburg was there, sitting on the window ledge and gripping it as if for support as he stared out into the square. When she crossed the room to his side she saw that his face was puffy and sagging and even his clothes reeked of cheap wine.

Only the wreckage of the feast remained at the table below. The chairs were empty. Across the deserted square the three old men were receding. Three thin backs, three round-crowned hats. The very tall old man was still in the middle, and as they played they bent their knees and shuffled from side to side in time to their music. Their legs looked so very thin . . . so very infirm . . . old men's legs . . . .

Freiburg reached unsteadily for Ursula and laid his head against her. She held him there, watching over his warm drunken chestnut head the three old men shuffling away into the dark shadows. Shuffle to the right, shuffle to the left. Like old bent sticks their legs seemed. Past the clock-tower . . . into the shadows . . . gone . . . .

Still she stayed in the window, holding Freiburg against her, listening, until she could no longer be sure whether she still heard the vibration of a thin, high note. (. . . how the wide mouth pursed suddenly tight over the reed . . . and the heavy curved eyelids opened, wide, over eyes rolled back in agony or ecstasy . . . .)

Freiburg's maudlin tears had soaked through her nightgown. She could feel them spreading hot and wet across her bosom, as if her heart had burst.

THE DYING DAY OF FRANCIS BAINSBRIDGE

*

by George Johnston

F rancis Bainsbridge could see his death coming from a long
way away.

He had seen it coming for a week now – ten days.

He had seen it in those strange moments of dizziness when
he bent over to tie up his shoes; in the nights, waking to the forlorn stillness with its endlessly receding perspective of silence,
feeling that inside his brain was a clenched fist all a-strain which
might suddenly fling its fingers wide. He had seen it when, in
coming too abruptly round a corner, he had found a vacuum
where once had been the accustomed pressures that held him
upright, and he had felt himself falling, falling, falling: the
whole being of him without weight or substance, toppling into
eternity. He had felt it in the prickling sweat of his palms, the
sudden foolish paralyses of shoulder or arm or hand that would
leave his grey fingers motionless above a scatter of coins on a café
table, locked in a bloodless parody of mime.

He had long since discounted the once-hopeful belief that it
was nothing but a passing illness: the seizures came with too
sinister a regularity, but always metronomic to the true pulse
of time.

Death came towards Francis Bainsbridge from a long way
away – not so far away now as a week ago – but at least it
was not this stupid fictitious death that *stalked* a man. It did
not slink along behind his meagre humanity: it had no need to

conceal its intentions. It came to meet him. It was only the past that stalked him.

He sipped his Gancia and stared past the shrill romping children in the Piazza della Rotonda, past the wet flat lip of the fountain bowl, past the *gelati* man with his red and white barrow, past the gossiping women, black-shawled already against the invading dusk. His eyes, glazed and vague with the span of his focus, sought death in the shadows mustering beneath the portico.

The Pantheon, huge, unrepentant, sullenly pagan beneath the timid little cross that still trapped the glitter of the sun, offered him nothing, neither the visibility of death nor the assurance of immortality. The eight columns, high and dusk-dark, rose to the sombre entablature with Agrippa's name still chiselled there after two thousand years, and then the great breast of the dome and the fragile cross shining as brightly as the single early star which winked a celestial irony beyond it. The insignificance of the cross reminded Bainsbridge of it again.

'It was a tiny cross, no bigger than a woman's forearm,' he said loudly, talking to nobody.

The young Italian at the next table glanced at him curiously, and Bainsbridge, intercepting his look, first glowered at him and then smiled.

'I'll swear *you* have never torn Christ from a cross with your own hands,' he said, beguilingly.

'*Buona sera, signor*,' the young man answered shyly, his voice soft, musical, embarrassed, and then he turned away and began to speak with a nervous gaiety to the plump, pretty girl who sat with him.

Bainsbridge shrugged and smiled secretly at the pale lemon gleam in his glass of vermouth. Let the fool moon into the bovine eyes of his Roman darling: he would never in his life again have the chance of knowing why a man should die – not just to die like a dog or a plant or an insect, but to have a *reason* for death.

In the square there was nobody else to whom he might talk.

There was a spiv pedlar, a vendor of ties, a square, metal-faced young man with a voice like the rattle of coins in a tin who shuffled about with his fibre suitcase open and his gaudy wares hanging down like the lolling tongues of dreamt dragons.

The sun struck the tip of the slender cross on the fountain obelisk and threw a triangle of light on a scabby edge of shops at the far corner of the square, where a bunch of tourists posed for a photograph, all smiling idiotically and shuffling about with stiff furtive glances over their shoulders to make sure that they were not obliterating the shop signs which some day, in five black pasteboard snapshot albums, would testify to their presence in Rome.

That's me there, they would say, pointing at the tawdry little grey-and-white oblongs fastened by their corners to the black pasteboard, *that's me there, I look awful, the sun was right in our eyes.* And by that time, of course, Bainsbridge would be dead, rotting, stewing in a pit.

He watched them go, hurrying, and he had a sense of queer triumph in the knowledge that he could stay here, quite motionless, hunched over his Gancia in the shadow of the Pantheon, knowing where they would go, knowing everything they would say. Up the Via dei Pastini to the Corso . . . *Come on, hurry, or we shall miss it!* . . . along the Via Tritone, Piazza Barberini . . . *Listen, do come on, we can see the fountains later* . . . up the Via Sistina to the piazza, looking out on the shadowy vale to the last shimmer of the sun on St Peter's dome. And then back again, giggling along the bright shops, pausing at the fountains, chattering their inanities. And Bainsbridge was with them, hovering around them, mocking, the grisly phantom in the fifteenth-century woodblack whispering of death.

He turned quickly, to measure the thought against the love-sick apathy of the neighbouring Italian, but he was still enthralled by his girl and Bainsbridge scowled at him. The young man

28

seemed to sense it, for he leant very close to the girl and took her plump hands in his and whispered to her tenderly.

Bainsbridge crumpled a thousand-lire note on the table and scraped his chair back. He knew that the Italian and the girl were staring at him, whispering, as he moved away.

Going up the steps of the Pantheon he scrutinised very carefully the deep wells of shadow behind each of the gloomy columns, but there was nothing there. In the square behind him the children, who shunned the sombre portico at sundown, chirped and squeaked their pointless play.

One of the massive studded doors was open, but he turned and peered back through the columns toward the café. They were still there, close together, lovesick, calfsick. Bainsbridge, entering the Pantheon, imagined that even from this distance he could smell the milk from the girl's great young tits.

Inside, the measureless gloom pressed down upon self-conscious altars, crushing them with a cruel, heedless magnificence, and the tiny pale needlepoints of flame at the candelabra trembled. Needlepoints. How many angels would dance on the point of those needles under the triumphant pressure of the pagan darkness? Needlepoint? Wasn't that what his wife used to do, years before, sitting by the fire, her thick mouth a tight wad of concentration? Needlepoint? No angels had danced for her, the bitch!

Bainsbridge stood just inside the door, in love with the darkness and the triumph of the older gods. This was the time to visit the Pantheon, to come at dusk when the ancient shadows crept back to hide the gilt and mock the plaques and subdue the desolate pale Madonnas. They could plant their little cross above its dome, and send its tiles away to adorn Byzantium, and a Vicar of Christ could steal its bronze to make his canopy. Oh yes, they could even try to obliterate its pagan harlotry under a soft name, a respectable name. *Santa Maria Rotonda*. It was still Hadrian's church, Agrippa's the older gods'.

A priest was shuffling towards him, holding the hand of a small boy cowed by the darkness.

'Here is a man of God,' Bainsbridge told himself happily. 'Let us put it to him.'

And when the priest came closer Bainsbridge moved across and barred his way, and the boy, who had not seen him in the shadows, jumped and choked back a scream, and then shrank closer to the reassurance of the black habit.

The priest frowned slightly.

'What penalty, father,' said Bainsbridge smiling, 'what penalty in death awaits one who has torn Christ from a cross?'

The priest stared at him, suddenly wide-eyed and fearful, as if he had glimpsed the devil, and then without a word he hurried past him to the door, his thin black figure thrown protectingly about the boy.

Outside the man cried '*Gelati*!' and rang his bell.

On the second step of the Pantheon death advanced a little closer to Francis Bainsbridge.

The fist was in his head, getting ready to spread its fingers, and the dizziness seemed to take the right half of his body away from him. But it returned it to him, and he went slowly around to the side of the Pantheon in case he wanted to be sick.

The old walls drove down here, reaching for their antique foothold deep in the heart of an older earth, so that the black wall made one side of a sort of dry moat, and down there in the litter and the foul smells the terrible cats of the Pantheon scavenged and scratched and fought among their stinking bits of fish and rubbish. And a beggar in a long pale coat leant against the railing and tossed dry crusts to them from a crumpled paper bag. Luminous eyes were down there in the pit, burning and sliding and flickering.

The beggar seemed oblivious to the stench rising from the chasm, to the howls of rage and terror and hunger, to the spit and crooning wail of lust from a narrow parapet just below him, where two gaunt, scarred beasts duelled for possession of a mangy, slit-eyed female.

But he turned at Bainsbridge's approach, his twisted figure falling by old usage into the servile stoop that marked his calling. The ingratiating whine rose automatically to his lips. To plead his poverty his withered face, under the sea-blue street lamp, offered sharp bones to the shadows and pallor to the light.

Exultantly, Bainsbridge studied the ancient suffering face of this man who was as close to death as he was – closer, surely? – and then he said to him, 'Come with me and eat.'

The beggar tilted the brown paper bag and the crusts fell into the pit with a dry rattle, and down below there were new hissings and scufflings and a single cry, shrill and terrible.

The two of them walked away together up the side street; they could hear the music in the little Neapolitan café.

Under the light, the beggar's head was resting now against the yellow-painted wall, just below the painted paunch of the fat monk. His eyes were glazed and he breathed heavily and his face was flushed with all the minestrone and pasta and scampi he had eaten and the Tuscan wine with which he had sluiced it down. Yet it was to the painted figure on the wall, not to the gorged and stertorous scarecrow opposite, that one looked for a picture of self-indulgence.

Bainsbridge liked the paintings. All the walls of the café were painted to simulate a very old religious fresco, blotched and peeling; but a second glance revealed that the monks and abbots, and even the saints and angels, were all lascivious, mischievous creatures enjoying profane delights. This figure of the stout, leering monk, for instance, with his hand inside the milkmaid's bodice, this was the very personification of lust and robust vitality. Resting against it, the beggar's face was nothing but a horrible old parchment, loose and rumpled, dredged of all life and purpose.

Look at him, Bainsbridge whispered to himself excitedly. *See, he is dying before my eyes!* A sudden panic gripped him. *Or is he already dead?* The thick breathing had stopped. There was no perceptible breathing at all. Coarse, puckered webs of flesh hooded the exhausted eyes. Bainsbridge could feel the dizzy sickness coming over him. It was unthinkable that the fool should die, like this, before he had even talked to him.

'Come now!' he said sharply. 'Wake up, wake up!'

With a great effort the old man opened his eyes, but the effort was at least enough to give him back what claim he had on life, for his manner was immediately obsequious again.

'Oh, forgive me, sir,' he whispered. 'Forgive me, sir, please. It is the wine.'

Bainsbridge leant back in his chair, content again, and in his trouser pocket his right hand fondled the thick roll of thousand-lire notes. More money by far than he or the derelict opposite was ever likely to need.

'Well, have more wine then,' he said, but there was a grudging edge to the invitation. There wouldn't be much point to it if the old fool got blind drunk or went idiotically to sleep again.

The beggar seemed to sense the situation, for he shook his head slowly, although in his eyes there was an expression of faint resentment that, by his own approval, any vestige of this fantastic bounty should be allowed to escape him.

'Another flask of wine,' said Bainsbridge quietly, 'will cost me one hundred and twenty lire.' He paused, and added without kindliness, 'Would you prefer the money to the wine?'

The beggar's eyes sharpened to glittering, covetous points. 'Well sir, if you mean it, I – '

'What good is money to you?' Bainsbridge cut in sharply.

The beggar shook his head vaguely, trying desperately to follow the idiosyncrasies of his benefactor's conversation; and then, assuming this to be an accusation of some sort, the professional whine crept back to his voice:

'A man must live, sir. Oh, I would work, sir, I *would*. But I am too old and too sick and there is no work for the likes of me. And yet a man must live, sir.'

'Live!' Bainsbridge sneered. The old humbug had responded exactly as he had meant him to. 'Sleeping in gutters, scavenging for scraps, snivelling at the coat-tails of the world and whining for its droppings. What reason is there for *you* to live?'

'Oh, as you say, sir. I am a miserable man and not much use to anybody.' The ingratiating smile touched his withered lips, exposing the black stumps of teeth. 'But what reason is there for me to die, sir?'

Bainsbridge smiled a little. What a question to have asked! Six weeks back he could have asked it of himself and cared nothing about the answer. In the warm certainty of existence, belonging then to all that lived, what had it *mattered*? Death was an ultimate abstraction, to be considered ultimately, but not while life flowed by. And then, quite suddenly, the unsuspected razor-edge of security had dissolved, without explanation, and there was death, the *reality* of death, coming towards him.

Even now he shuddered, remembering, recalling how terror at first had elbowed reason from his mind. Yes, he had panicked in the beginning, whimpered with the fear that threatened to smother him with its choking blackness. How paradoxical that in fighting against it, and subduing it, his reason had found salvation not in any *reasonable* thing at all, but in something which, before the fear, his intelligence would have rejected out of hand. What he had found, quite simply, was a reason *why* he had to die. True, he had found it entangled in some occult mystery which even now he did not clearly understand. That didn't matter any longer. Having the reason was the important thing. It was unnecessary to seek the explanation.

And now this old fool opposite wanted to know what reason there was for him to die. For *him*? He was hard put to it not to laugh aloud. Did the scarecrow think the whole world was a garden and all the clods were flowers?

And when the scarecrow did die, what would the world lose

in losing it? A street nuisance the less, a bundle of stinking rags to be destroyed in the public incinerator. Any pariah dog or alley cat would go as grandly.

In a moment or two he would explain all this to him. It would be amusing to see if he could understand the difference – the gigantic difference – between them.

In the back of his mind the music went on, the fat waiter with a violin tucked beneath his shining chins and the two young men playing accordions, and the music went dancing along behind his brain like sunbeams in a Naples street, the chords and the laughter and the red smiles of the musicians all tangled up with the flicker of fat fingers across the strings and the smell of cheese and garlic and wine.

The beggar had returned to his plate now, picking at the scraps. Bainsbridge watched him contemptuously. The high-domed forehead running into the cropped yellow skull he had mistaken for the residue of wisdom or intelligence: it was no more than an echoing, bony chamber containing the shrivelled peppercorn of a brain. It was a charity even to admit the existence of a brain. To suggest the possibility of its harbouring a soul or a reason was pure absurdity. The beggar poked an explora-tory finger at a scrap of scampi in its cold batter. He pushed it to the rim of the plate, rolling it over, and then picked it up and swallowed it. Bainsbridge thought of the thin acrid juices of the old, ruined body seizing on the greasy gobbet and making life of it.

Yes, but for how long? It was only on the point of *reason* that one could accept the fact that he, Francis Pitt Bainsbridge, and this pitiful carcass were probably pretty much the same distance away from death. It was perfectly logical that there *should* be a reason for his own death. He was not half the beggar's age, he had always looked after himself, in his own way he had served humanity well enough, he had many things yet to live for. Why, if it had not been for the little Christ hanging on his cross . . . .

Coming down from the Arlberg in the bright sun with the meadow smell, and there it was by the side of the road – the little Christ, all tortured and twisted, hanging on its nails in the bright blue box. And when he had stopped the car and walked back to the wayside shrine he had seen the wonderful agony in the carven face, and the wood as brown as desert skin and chiselled by somebody who had felt something . . . .

When Bainsbridge had come over the Brenner into Italy, the Customs man had seen the little Christ in the boot, but he had given it only a contemptuous glance, as if it had been some trumpery tourist souvenir, and tossed it disdainfully aside and rummaged in the bags for cigarettes or liquor or Swiss watches. And then he had boredly waved him on, down into Italy with its multitude of Christs, and Lippi's painting in the Uffizi with three nails and the crown of thorns on the white cloth . . . . Still, he must have felt a twinge of guilt at the Customs man having seen it, because he had pulled the car in to the side of the road before he had gone ten miles, and walked through a meadow thick with daisies to where a clear stream sluiced down, and there he had wrenched the little Christ away from the cross, which was of inferior wood and cracked, and then he had carried the little figure back to the car in his pocket and wrapped it very carefully in one of his nylon shirts . . . .

The beggar was licking his finger and studying Bainsbridge patiently.

'Are you a Christian?' Bainsbridge asked him.

The beggar made as if to answer, with the ready servility with which apparently he responded to any question; but then he paused, his eyes wary, and in the end he said nothing.

Bainsbridge watched him cynically, aware of what was running through the old man's mind. He could not afford to offend his benefactor, that was it, and it was not always easy in this holy city, this city of God, with the Communist slogans plastered over the walls and God living in his big palace on the other side of the Tiber, it was not always easy to know where offence might lie. How easy it was now to be ashamed of being a Christian: in Rome of all places, and to have to be cautious about confessing such a thing eighteen centuries after the catacombs and the persecutions and the blood of martyrs.

'Oh, come now,' Bainsbridge said sharply, to give the fool a lead, 'surely you believe in God?'

'God. Ah, yes, sir,' the beggar whispered quickly. 'In God of course, sir.'

But his old eyes were still shifty, uneasy, and this made Bainsbridge angry so that he was on the point of asking the fellow if he gave thanks to his God for his rags and scraps and the wretched life he lived in the unfriendly streets. He resisted the impulse: it would probably only bewilder him and reduce him to a state of such imbecility that he would be totally unreceptive to the important things he had to tell him. And it *was* important that this old man, so close to death himself and with so little reason for it, should know that his host, too, was dying – but with reason. Yes, *with reason*.

'And you believe in Jesus?' He put the question absently, not even hearing the beggar's answer, for his mind was engaged again with thoughts of the little Christ.

In the beginning, when the illness had first come to him, he had not connected it with his theft of the crucifix. It was later, much later, that he had discovered the significance in the fact that the first faint tremors had come to him that afternoon in the hills above Bolzano, driving down after lunch from the bright meadow where he had torn the little figure from the cross. But not at first. Why should it have occurred to him? He was a rational man, intelligent, not one given to childish, superstitious fears.

Indeed, weeks had passed between that afternoon and the day of realisation. The seizures had grown more frequent, sometimes quite frightening; but he had blamed the rich food he had eaten, poor wines and the change of water, the fatigues of travel added to an out-of-sorts liver. And the doctor he had seen in Florence had made the same diagnosis, and given him capsules which had not been of the slightest use.

Yet something, even then, had driven him with a sort of frenzy to seek out churches, to plunge into galleries, to scour through guide-books. Bolzano, Verona, Venice, Padua, Siena, Pisa, Florence, San Gimignano, Orvieto, Rome. At first he had gone complacently, seeking out the Crucifixions to compare them with his own wonderful little wooden Christ, returning to his hotel jubilant that none could match it for its poignancy and terror. And he would prop it against the cheap hotel dressing-table and study it with admiration, and wonder about the unknown village genius of the Tyrol who had carved it with such passion and sincerity.

And then one night in Siena, in a little *pensione* right next to the black and white cathedral, the vertigo had struck him so fiercely that he had fallen in his bathroom, and that night he had slept fitfully through terrible broken nightmares in which all the crucifixes in the world surrounded him, hemming him in like a vast, dark forest, and he was crushed beneath the weight of all those twisted bodies dragging down, hanging on the nails. How terrible it had been to feel the *weight* of Christ dragging, dragging . . . . He had awakened before dawn, bathed in sweat, knowing that he would die.

But even then, with the hideous memory of the night still clawing into his brain, the same demon had still scourged him on, driving him to the paintings and the shrines and the altars. He was sick, filled with revulsion and terror, reeling on and on through a terrifying landscape, sombre and golden and aflame — Calvary, Gethsemane, Golgotha, Judgment Days and open pits, pillars of fire and grim-faced archangels, the whirl of cherubim and the bony claws of death. And then, one day, a sort of peace had come to him in front of a quite ordinary little crucifix – the sort of thing they turned out by the lorry-load in Volterra – in a little church in a village of which he did not even know the name. It was not peace at first, but a sort of fierce, tremendous excitement at knowing *why*, an excitement that lifted him, buoyant, upon a wave of pride and ecstasy. At first he had suspected that it might be nothing but a defensive mechanism against the terror which for days had beset him, justification for his own egotism, a form of vainglory; but then the peace had come to calm him. And after that it had been easier, so much easier, knowing the *reason* why he had to die.

There had been, of course, that final lapse into cowardice, into a panic that was desperate and unreasoning, but it had not lasted long, not more than one night. In the morning his intelligence had reasserted itself and there had been no more trouble.

It had come to him, trying to sleep, that he *could* save himself. It had seemed so simple, lying in the sweat-damp sheets, sick and feverish with relief. All he had to do was to get rid of the little Christ, hurl it into the hedges beside some lonely road, toss it into a river as he was driving over a bridge. He had felt very weak but deliriously happy then, realising the absurd simplicity of the solution. He had even joked about it, talking aloud in the darkness about 'exorcising the evil spirit' and 'casting out the demon', and then laughing uncontrollably at the irony of the inversion.

But later, when the moon went down and the night grew very dark and still and all the town around him was crouched in a deathly silence on its hill, he had lain there without a sound, shivering in his sweat and frightened, watching the little Christ propped against the big brass bowl which the chambermaid had filled with *petit-angelo*. Although the room was very dark – nothing now but pale stars to light it – he could quite clearly see every scored line and sharp plane in the suffering face, each stretched sinew in the dragging body.

In the morning, with his breakfast coffee, he had drunk brandy to pull himself together, and he had seen, of course, that neither the fear nor the solace of the night could be related to logic. That some strange destructive aura clung to the little Christ figure he could no longer doubt. But the transmission of this malevolence to himself had been brought about by its *theft*: the continuance or otherwise of *possession* could not affect it one way or another. To throw the Christ away now would be merely to confess his cowardice, to succumb to unreason, to add immeasurably to the original guilt, and – at this he smiled to himself – to deprive himself of something rare and beautiful which he had come to prize beyond anything he had ever owned. It was better, he had told himself, to *go quietly*. This resurgence of his sense of values had given him all the encouragement he had needed. After that it had been all right.

Bainsbridge shook his head quickly. He could feel the sweat cold on his forehead. And as the face of the beggar came back into the focus of his eyes he said, almost as if he were speaking to himself, 'And do you believe in the power of Christ to punish for . . . ?'

But the beggar was not listening. His face was wax-pale and his eyes afraid and he had pushed his chair to one side and was beginning to edge away from the table.

'Sit down!' Bainsbridge shouted. 'I want to talk to you. Sit down, I say!' He closed his eyes and took hold of himself. The fist was in his head again, flexing its fingers. 'More drink. Yes, that's it, more drink.' His right hand dug into his pocket and he tossed the big bundle of banknotes on to the table. 'Yes, yes, we shall have more to drink. Where is that bloody waiter? Waiter! More wine! *Waiter!*'

The sweat was boiling on his forehead now, and his mouth

and nostrils were choking with a foul stench, and the back of his neck was chill as ice. The table with its greasy emptied dishes and the bulbous yellow head of the beggar and the rumpled heap of banknotes were curling away and down, all together, sliding in a great descending arc, slowly falling away from him . . . .

'*Prego, signore? Perdoni se l'ho fatta aspett ar tanto* . . . .'

Bainsbridge blinked his eyes and it all fell back into place again. The fat waiter was there beside him, whispering insinuatingly, the violin strangling in his pudgy hand, the soiled handkerchief still tucked beneath his polished chins, a bottle of white wine resting in the crook of his arm, like a baby. He was smiling. A servile smile, yet nervous, uneasy. Had he shouted too loudly? Made a scene? Did he look ill? The beggar was smiling, too, baring all his horrible black fangs and stumps. But they were not smiling at *him*! They were looking at him, yes, but they were smiling down at the scatter of money strewn across the soiled cloth.

They would smile for ever, their filthy obsequious smiles not for him but for that! It was their continuity, their reason. What did his reason for death matter to them, who had no reason for dying? All the reason they had, for *anything*, was there on the table in front of them.

The lire notes all seemed to leap together, like a crazy film running backwards, to mount higher and higher into a gigantic pale column with the two terrible smiles hovering around it, watching it grow.

With an effort that seemed to paralyse half his body, Bainsbridge regained his control. His hands were shaking and wet with sweat, but he reached out and took the money up and returned it to his pocket, smiling triumphantly at the other smiles. But the task had forced him to relax his grip on the thing inside his head. One of the fingers seemed to stir, touching the substance of his brain with pain, probing at its casing, letting in the light. A terrible light, cold and limitless, carrying to his dulled senses its hollow revelation. He was dying. He was dying, just like anybody else. The little wooden Christ had nothing to do with it . . . nothing . . . nothing.

The words of the smiling waiter, offering the slim bottle, seemed to come to him from a great distance, from the ultimate remoteness of the desolation:

'It is a very popular wine, sir . . . speciality of Napoli . . . sweet and delicate, from the lower slopes of Vesuvius . . . *Lacryma Christi*. The visitors always enjoy to drink the Tears of Christ, eh?'

Bainsbridge pushed back, and the chair went over with a clatter and he staggered to the door and was gone into the darkness. The waiter watched him go, open-mouthed. For a moment the beggar was immobile, paralysed by terror, aghast that he had been abandoned, with the bill still unpaid after all he had drunk and eaten. And then he wriggled past the waiter and fled into the street, screaming.

Gasping, almost blinded by sweat, Bainsbridge ran wildly, stumbling, reeling from side to side, hearing the wild screams and the slap and slither of the feet behind him, and knowing that it was death that pursued him.

The Pantheon was just ahead, black and old and impassive against the callous stars. He tripped on the first step, picked himself up again, staggered higher and flung himself moaning at the oblivious stones, beating at them with his fists, tearing at them with his fingers.

And then everything collapsed from beneath him and he felt himself falling away to one side, falling, falling, as the invisible fingers in his head suddenly flung themselves wide like five prongs of fire; and his own fingers, dragging slowly down the stones, left five vertical threads of blood, bright and slender as silk.

In the pit below the cats leapt upon him, spitting and clawing, and then wailed shrilly and fled in terror, arching their backs, their baleful eyes flashing and flickering, green and sulphur-yellow, from the ledges and corners.

The crowd had thickened by the time they dragged his body

to the pavement and stretched it on the lower step beneath the dark blank mystery of the portico. The beggar had fled, but all the Piazza della Rotonda was seething with it.

The old priest knelt beside the dusty figure, spattered now with filth, and felt carefully inside the coat to ascertain what he already knew – that the heart was still. But his hand encountered something hard and thin and twisted, and carefully he withdrew from the inner pocket the little wooden Christ, and he looked at if for a long moment before laying it reverently on the stones beside the body.

An old woman in a black shawl, standing in the front of the crowd, clapped hands to her eyes and wailed, but the priest looked up at her and shook his head with a gentle smile and said, 'There is no reason for grief, mother. He is with God.'

WILD EMPEROR

*

by Charmian Clift

In the best room of the *Gasthof zum Engel* Harry Piggott
awakened reluctantly. He clenched his eyelids against the
morning light – the clear, cold, still-feared mountain
light – trying to go back, to sink.... Where? What had he
dreamed?

Beside him Doris stirred in her sleep, and Piggott's eyes
opened wide. In the very centre of the white warm cocoon of
embroidered sheets and bundled feathers her live breath burnt
like a small slow fire against his ribs, and all down the length of
his tense, distrustful body her body lay against him, soft and
vulnerable in sleep.

'Well!' Piggott whispered, and then, on a sudden cry of
conviction: 'Oh, Doris lass!'

But as he turned towards her, his arms already gathering,
folding, memory at last came back, and guiltily he drew away
from her. He was normally a moderate man.

'It was storing it up, like,' he told himself defensively. 'Not
knowing from one day to next whether she'd come or whether
not. Had a chap been certain all along there wouldn't have been
such cause for bother.'

But the bother burnt inside him still, shameful and insistent,
and after a while he edged quietly out of bed, pushing aside the
billowing white eiderdown very carefully so as not to wake her.
In the long rectangle of the window the sky pulsed with light

as the great peaks, still snow-capped, caught the sun. Piggott grinned suddenly, and walked barefoot to the little carved balcony, forgetting his usual furtive glance at the dark Christ hanging in the corner of the whitewashed room.

The old fiery wood of the balcony rail curved damp and smooth beneath his hands and the clean chill of the morning hit across his face so that his quick gasp was as much pain as pleasure. For a moment he considered waking Doris to share the dawn with him, her very first Tyrolean sunrise. But he was reluctant yet to meet those round, surprised blue eyes, and besides – he rationalised quickly – the poor lass would scarcely thank him for dragging her out of bed just to look at a sunrise when she'd been travelling half across Europe for the last two days. His face was still hot and he was grateful for the cold air on it as he leant out across the balcony. The chill would bring him back to normality, like a cold tub at home. Nothing like it first thing.

Below in the cherry orchard the mist looped insubstantial garlands among the blossom that burst like thick foam across the hill; and under the trees, moving through the morning, the housekeeper Kathi climbed slowly from the shrine at the bottom of the orchard.

Her big limbs, heavy yet with sleep, dragged in the steaming grass, and as she came towards him she stooped among the trees, adding to the blue drift of forget-me-nots held against the billow of her breast. Beyond the orchard and the spindly hay huts poking up in the grey home meadow seven plumes of smoke were rising above the village huddled against the pine-dark hill: in the loop of the river the cotton mill sprawled pale and ghostly among the birches. As the peaks turned rose and gold in the sun the whole long valley, winding away south-westward to meet the inn, brimmed with light, and the needle-spired church perched precariously above the village shone in a sudden vehemence of white.

44

'It'll be a champion day,' Piggott murmured happily. 'Champion!'

Kathi, tranquil after paying her morning respects to the Mother of God, looked up and saw him on the balcony, leaning far out over the hanging sign of the golden angel. His short, stocky figure seemed so alien under the old carved eaves, his round face staring down at her above the rumpled collar of his striped flannelette pyjamas, that she laughed suddenly, showing her fine white teeth, and called to him, her voice carrying rich and full across the orchard.

'*Grüss Gott*, Herr Piggott! See, I have picked flowers for your wife before the sun is on them.'

He bent towards her, his face puckered anxiously in his effort to understand, and Kathi held the flowers for him to see and called again, the English queer and heavy on her tongue:

'Flowers, for your wife.'

'*Danke schön*, Kathi,' he called awkwardly, warmed as always by Kathi's kindness. 'She will be pleased.'

Kathi had come to rest by the inn door, and now she stood placidly in the wet grass, her wide pale face held up to him, as though her head was dragged back by the weight of the coiled brown hair. She was a woman in her early thirties, and although her body had thickened she retained the miraculously clear complexion of the mountain women, and a sort of large calm beauty that was so much a part of the eternal, expansive beauty of hill and stream, mountain and meadow that it did not compel attention. But Piggott, whose awakening had perhaps heightened particular perceptions, looked down on her and thought with a vehemence surprising in a moderate man: 'That Joseph's a fool if he doesn't have her.'

Kathi, misunderstanding his frown, called anxiously: 'You were comfortable, Herr Piggott? Your wife? She slept well?'

Her eyes were fixed upon him in such grave, deliberate inquiry that Piggott, forming a stumbling answer in German, was disconcerted, faltered, gave it up, and called rather too loudly, in English: 'Still asleep, Kathi. Long journey. Very tired. Everything strange. *Strange.* You understand, lass? Strange and new.'

Inside the room Doris lay curled into a tight bundle under the bedclothes, listening to the faltering conversation outside the window. Quite incomprehensible conversation, queer and dream-like and filled with gurglings and hissings: a thick stew of unknown sounds plopping and running together, with an occasional explosion of familiar words so surprising in their ordinariness that she could not attach meanings to them.

Her round blue eyes surveyed the room: the low ceiling leaping with reflected light; the plain whitewashed walls; the massive carved chest and wardrobe, whose door had swung open to reveal her new green travelling coat hanging limply over Harry's check jacket; her open suitcases on the floor, still packed neatly with their tissue-folded bundles . . . . 'Leave it till morning, love,' he had said, and his face had been hot, red, close to her own. She looked away quickly and met the anguished eyes of the black Christ, and for a moment she was held in a sort of fearful fascination, as if expecting bloody tears to ooze down the carved cheeks and the chiselled lips to open upon a cry of desolation. Under the bed-coverings she hugged her knees tighter and turned her head on the embroidered pillow so that she could see the window, flung wide to the mountains, and Harry's broad hunched back framed in it, incongruously ordinary against the aspiring peaks that leapt and quivered as the sun struck them.

'He's got fat,' she thought, and looked above him to the mountains.

When Piggott came in from the balcony, creeping self-consciously across the bare boards, she was so still that for a moment he thought her asleep. And when she looked at him he was disconcerted – unprepared, somehow – by those two round eyes, China blue like a doll's, that gave to Doris's small peaked face an extraordinary startled expression. It was a look, usually, which awakened in him an odd tenderness, deep and protective, which always seemed to reassure him — as long as he could keep his eyes away from her hair, spread like a tawny tumbled scarf on the pillow, and his memory from the feel of those little thin bones under his hands. 'Like a bird's bones,' he thought, and then, blustering to himself, angry, betrayed: 'Damn it all, she's my *wife*!'

Uneasily he moved to the bed and with awkward heartiness pinched her cheek. 'Well, love?'

'Harry!' she whispered incredulously. 'Harry, you never told me about the mountains.'

'Course I didn't, lass!' His heartiness was suddenly unaffected. 'Told you the mill was in the bloody Sahara desert!' He grinned, relieved, humouring her. 'Wrote you pages about the bloody mountains. Here, who reads my letters then if you don't, eh? Daft little loon you are. Did you expect Austria to look like North Prospect Road then? Or Bradford on a Saturday night? Eh?' He grinned, pleased, paternal, pinching her, the little loon.

'But you never told me,' she cried from the pillow, her great startled eyes fixed on him, 'that mountains were like *this* . . . like . . . . Harry, what are their names? That tall one. It was *red*, Harry. A minute ago it was red, and it lifts up so high . . . strong . . . .'

'Aye,' Harry said. 'They're queer colours of mornings. Queer. You never get used to 'em, quite. But search me if they have names, love. Never occurred to me to ask.'

He scratched his head perplexedly, peering out the window, peering at the mountains, as if expecting to see labels on their dazzling slopes. 'Why,' he said finally, 'I've been so busy, lass — what with the machinery and all, and teaching these chaps difference between a bobbin and a thumbscrew . . . and . . . and worrying about you . . . .'

His fingers were touching her hair, feeling the deep red of it like flames licking his hand.

Worrying about her. In the nights. The long, cold nights.

The cold, unearthly silence of the nights when the stars glittered in the frost and the window was crowded with the mountains and the wash of the moon. Mountains with no names. But there. Always there.

'I've missed you, Doris,' he said, thickly, the warm red lapping him. 'You don't mind your old man that much, eh, love?' But her head was turned away from him, and her eyes were fixed on the mountains, as if she had made an incredible discovery. Piggott disentangled his fingers from her hair and said, very bluff and uneasy, 'Well, let's get down to breakfast, then. I'll slip down to mill after, while you're unpacking your things.'

'But are you going to the mill this morning?' She looked childish and uncertain again, even perhaps a little afraid.

Piggott swelled, warmed, patted her briskly. 'Job comes first, love. I'll be back lunchtime to show you round a bit. Come now. That's the lass.'

It had been some weeks now since the round stove of green majolica tiles had been lit in the low white communal eating room, but from habit Piggott still took his meals at a scrubbed table placed close to the stove. Old Kresten and the taciturn Josef were already seated, breaking rolls and drinking strong coffee from great blue cups, and from the low doorway that led to the inn yard and the fragrant outbuildings Kathi came, struggling with a big wicker basket piled high with rolled and dampened linen. Inside the doorway she put the basket down and stood for a moment, blinking, still snared in a yellow net of sunlight. Through her white lawn sleeves the shape of her arms showed pink and solid, and her breast panted with exertion, shedding rivulets of sunshine.

Old Kresten watched her, lifting his gross Roman head and wiping daintily with a red cotton handkerchief at his lips, full and dark and curiously silky under the spreading white curtain of moustache. Beside him, Josef looked only at the scrubbed surface of the table and the sweet white bread crumbling in his twisted fingers. The old man sighed, finished his coffee in gusty sucking gulps, and eased back in his chair, so that the sun was warm on his neck and his great paunch rested comfortably between spread thighs. He considered his guests, but remotely, from behind a wall of pride. Beside him he was conscious of the hard nervous fingers crumbling distractedly at little heaps of bread, and this consciousness was like a secret wound in him that the strangers must not see.

'Eh, Herr Piggott,' he said genially, but still from behind his wall of pride, 'we will have to look after the little wife, eh? She must put flesh on her bones. Look what a fine figure of a man you have become after two months only. Nearly as fine as me, eh?' His chuckle was deep, rich. 'We must do the same for the wife, or you will think me a bad host.' And he smiled at the little pale bird-like thing who stared at him with such huge, astonished eyes: embracing her with kindliness in the old loose-lipped male sureness of his smile. But she only looked at him dazzled, uncomprehending; and beside her the fat, red-faced husband let his jaws relax on a mouthful of ham as his face puckered in an anxiety to understand.

Old Kresten's eyelids drooped contemptuously, but he smiled still, the genial, dark-lipped smile lifting back from broken brown stumps of teeth, waiting for the comprehension to come to Piggott's face. Oh, a good little man, Herr Piggott. Better than some English he had known, and clever with machines, it was said. But alien. As the machines were alien. And the new hard curves of the mill. Kresten tried to allow for the mill. It was needed: times had not been good since the war; seasons bad, prices soaring, even the tourists kept away by the money restrictions. And the young men restless, unsure, sighing for cinemas and motorcycles and far-off cities, or perhaps just for the lost carelessness of days when the old ways had seemed good enough, and satisfying. Yes, yes. It was wrong to resent Herr Piggott because of the mill. Perhaps with steady work and the price of a litre or two of wine in the pockets of their leather breeches the young men might lift their heads again and sing as they used to sing, and make the maidens happy in the hay. The old man laughed silently, richly, feeling the sun on his neck, remembering. One would regret the slaughtered grove of birches, of course, and that wide sunny wilderness where the river fanned out below the cataract; where, long ago, he had walked with the big singing girl from the Vorarlberg who had never returned to her own people after he had kissed her by the river. Anna. Anna, who had sung the high, wild Vorarlberg songs as she burnished and baked in the *Gasthof* kitchen. Anna, who had borne him four great sons and grown stout and comfortable before she gave that long last bewildered sigh that still haunted him at night, and closed her eyes. As if, even then, she could not believe that the war had swallowed them. Hans, Ernst, Wilhelm. And Josef . . . .

The twisted fingers were drumming on the table, scattering the snowy piles of bread, and Kresten's secret wound throbbed behind his armour of age and pride.

Piggott was laughing delightedly, understanding at last.

He turned to his wife, translating the old man's sally. 'How do you like being a *Frau*, lass? Eh? He's a great old chap, you'll see. Full of jokes. Champion old fellow. Champion!'

'Yes,' said Doris, smiling uncertainly. 'Yes, but ask him about the mountains, Harry. Ask him the name of the big one.' In the sunny square of the window, where forget-me-nots hung in a blue mist over a bright copper jug, she could see it still, the strong enduring flanks of it, sombre with forest, and the glittering peak raised pure and high.

Piggott asked the question haltingly, humouring her, the queer little loon. And the landlord, surprised, looked again at Doris, and answered wonderingly:

'Why, Herr Piggott, it is *Wildekaiser*, of course.'

'*Wildekaiser*? What does *Wildekaiser* mean?' Doris cried breathlessly, confused, and, strangely, it was Josef who answered her, lifting his dark head painfully, his nervous fingers quiet at last amid the doughy ruin of his breakfast roll.

'It means . . . .' He paused, his mouth writhing, his eyes dark with effort as he sought for the English words. 'It means . . . Wild Emperor.'

'Wild Emperor,' she whispered to herself. 'Wild Emperor.' And for the rest of the meal she could not keep her eyes away from Josef. He seemed to her like some carved creature, dark and worn, and with a sort of polished grain to the harsh folded cheeks and the craggy nose. And his hair seemed carved — coarse short swirls pressing upon the high thin brow; and the brown column of his throat showing in the neck of a faded flannel shirt. Only his hands and his eyes seemed alive to her: the hands restless and downed with fine black hair; the eyes dark and distracted with suffering. 'Wild Emperor,' she whispered to herself, thinking of the mountains.

After breakfast Piggott went off to the mill, his kiss embarrassed and perfunctory under the steadfast scrutiny of old Kresten, and she went up to her room in a sort of daze, scarcely realising what she was doing as she began to unpack the suitcases.

Kathi knocked timidly, bearing her gift of morning forget-me-nots in a creamy stone jar patterned in blue, and after she had presented them she still lingered, curious about the little English wife and the English clothes flung carelessly about the room.

'I will help,' she said finally. 'You do not mind, Frau Piggott?' Her big white hands stroked a crepe dress trimmed with black beads. Then she laughed suddenly and held it up against herself, giggling a little, fascinated as a child by the smallness of it and the beads worked in a pattern down the front. 'It is pretty . . . so pretty. Very nice.' She laughed, stroking the stuff tenderly. 'Everyone will stare when you wear it.'

The blood burnt at Doris's ears and her eyes started wide.

'But . . . but I don't . . . .' she cried helplessly. 'I didn't . . . Harry . . . Mr Piggott . . . he didn't tell me what to *bring*!' The crepe dress looked hideous, tawdry, incongruous against Kathi's simple dark skirt and bodice, and the fine white blouse.

'It is good you have come,' Kathi said simply, beginning methodically to fold and slip the jackets and dresses on to frilly padded hangers with little hanging sachets of lavender. 'Now Herr Piggott will be happy, and the machines they will be nice for him and soon the mill will work, and.... Oh, this – it is so pretty, Frau Piggott! This scarf with the little pictures. I know ... from other pictures in books. The Tower of London, eh? Windsor Castle. *Schloss*, we say. West ... Munster ... Abbey.'

Kneeling beside the suitcase, Doris felt it creep up in her cold and slow – the fear, the desolation. Four weeks, Harry had said. Four weeks. She could see his writing still, the thick black scrawl, wheedling, unsteady with his longing, and could feel again her own apathy, reading it over and over, vague with indecision, and the eyes of the old woman, Harry's mother, watching her slyly. 'Looks like I'll get through here four to five weeks' time, barring accidents that is,' he wrote. 'Aren't you proud of your old man, lass? It is very pretty here now, not cold at all now the snow has melted on the low ground, and I daresay we can spare a bit of brass now my prospects are so good, and there'll be the bonus and all. What about a bit of a holiday in the Tyrol, love, for last four weeks before job packs up?'

Four weeks. Just four weeks! Desolate, she crouched beside the suitcase, seeing the wall of mountains hung now with soft white cloud and seeming to have receded for miles, and *Wildekaiser* shouldering strong against the rest.

'Has anyone ever climbed it?' she asked Kathi. 'That one – *Wildekaiser*?'

'Why, yes, Frau Piggott.' Kathi paused in her folding, surprised. 'Often. It is not a difficult mountain. Herr Kresten – that is the landlord, as you will know – he was the first, I think, who climbed it, as a young man. He was a fine climber. The best climber in the valley. And his sons – all of them, often. He used to take them up with him when they were quite small. And after they climbed it many, many times, before the war they were – how do you say it? – guides. In the summer the tourists come. That is how we all speak a little English. Herr Kresten, too – but he will not, only *very* seldom – and the boys were guides.'

'Are they . . . ?' Doris began, and broke off in embarrassment. Kathi was turned away, busy over an open drawer.

'It was the war,' she said indistinctly, a little breathless. The drawer seemed to be sticking. She hammered it with the butt of her hand. 'They were killed. Hans. Ernst. Wilhelm. All but Josef. He was a prisoner. For many years.'

Doris could feel a pulse in her throat beating, beating. She felt queerly elated, aching, excited, terrified of asking further questions, yet unable to stop herself. 'Is . . . is Josef a guide now?' she asked.

'Now? Not now, Frau Piggott.' Kathi had at last succeeded in closing the drawer with a thud, but she still knelt there, her back turned to Doris. 'Not now.' And then she turned, rising to her feet, and took up the last garment from the bed and slipped it very carefully on to the hanger, smoothing the shoulders across and across with her big hands. Her face was placid and resigned.

'Why?' But Doris must know. She felt she must. She must. She urged in a little high, strained voice. 'Why has he stopped being a guide?'

Kathi adjusted the collar of the dress on the hanger. There was nothing in her face to show what she was thinking.

'He is afraid,' she said at last.

Behind her face, Doris could see the carved Christ, hanging above the red and yellow ears of maize, and at his feet the tumbled scarf with the London pictures.

She walked across and picked it up quickly and folded it and offered it to the housekeeper. 'I wish you'd have this, if you like it,' she said. 'Harry said you'd been so kind.'

Then Kathi laughed again and turned the scarf over in her hands, delighted, exclaiming with pleasure. When she had gone Doris went out to the balcony to watch for Harry coming back from the mill. 'She's in love with Josef!' she thought, with sudden conviction, and all at once she felt small and dizzy and afraid, leaning out above the golden angel, hanging high and lonely above the brimming valley, where the morning, caught in the chill bowl of mountains, shimmered in hot yellow silence. Yet it was not silence, for sounds came indistinctly, hanging lazy in the air. It was very difficult to tell whether they were close to the inn or very far away: a child laughing, the sharp insect-buzz of a saw, the half-human questioning plaint of the two goats tethered in the orchard, a little swinging peal of bells. Her eyes were on the distant mountains when Piggott came up from the mill, so that she did not see him until he called up to her from the grass below.

He had discarded his checked jacket. His face was shiny pink with sweat and his plumpness seemed to sag around him.

For lunch, Kathi brought them soup and trout fresh from the river and small rich cakes to eat with their coffee. Doris found it difficult to eat because of the thin face of Josef lowered over his meal. The abstracted, affectionate pat of Harry's plump hand on her knee made her tremble.

He finished the last of the cakes and wiped the back of his hand across his mouth. 'Ah,' he said, grinning, 'think of that food in England, eh?'

'Where will you take me this afternoon, Harry?' she asked.

'Oh, poor lass! An' the first day and all!' He was hurt with disappointment, anxious, pleading for forgiveness. 'Ah, the daft loons they've given me mucked up job this morning, and

I'm all of a bother, lass, to get it set right. Hold us up a fort-night if I can't get it right. Oh yes, good enough chaps they are. Happy – like kids. But if they'd think about job, think of what they're doing sometimes instead of their bloody mountains and who can climb them quickest and what someone's lass did behind a bloody haystack . . . .' He broke off embarrassedly and darted a half-furtive, half-apologetic glance toward Josef. 'There, love,' he went on, more calmly, 'I just can't get away this after-noon, and that's a fact.' And, touching her knee under the table, he added softly, intimately, 'I'll make it up, lass. You trust your old man.'

His hand curved and squeezed, hot, heavily caressing.

'It's all right, Harry,' Doris said sharply. 'I'll walk a bit. It's . . . it's all new to me. It doesn't matter where I go . . . which way.'

Josef lifted his gaunt head and looked at them for a moment. 'I go this afternoon to the high pasture,' he said. It was harsh, painful, the words pulled out of him separately as though each one hurt. 'If . . . .' His eyes were on her, bewildered. 'If the frau would be pleased to come, I will try to show her some of our valley.'

Doris said irresolutely, 'Why . . . well, I don't . . .'; but Piggott beamed, all relief and heartiness. 'Now that's a good chap, Josef. That's a champion idea. Of course she'll go.' And Kathi smiled, hovering about Josef, and said wistfully, 'You must show her the ruin, Josef. She will like the ruin.' And when the matter was explained to old Kresten he smiled also, fingering his moustache, although his eyelids drooped a little. Doris was afraid of the landlord, sensing his aloofness and the small hard core of contempt embedded deep and incorruptible under his genial pleasantries. But it was decided, out of her hands, and so she whispered, not looking at Josef, 'Thank you very much. I'd like to.'

They left the *Gasthof* with the two goats from the orchard skipping and trotting ahead of them. 'You do not mind?' he had asked, untethering them.

And she loved them; their thin black faces and yellow eyes and their horns curved high like curious shells; and their legs so thin and brittle-looking, skipping about on tiny polished hoofs; and the way their tails flicked derisively. They were wonderful creatures, unreal. She was like a child, wanting to touch them, but they trotted away from her, feet rattling, tails a-quiver.

They took the muddy track that led down through the village, where the rows of maize cobs glowed under the dark eaves, and the smell of wood and dung rose pungent from cavernous doorways. Women in kerchiefs and aproned skirts were gathered at the water trough, filling their pails beneath the gaudy, bright-painted statue of St Florian with his own little pail held high under the overhanging branch of a cherry-tree, old and blossom-heavy.

'*Grüss Gott*,' the women called, very courteous, and holding in their interest and excitement.

'*Grüss Gott*!' Josef replied quietly as he passed St Florian. And Doris, following him, was suddenly bold, and a tremulous smile touched her mouth as she whispered '*Grüss Gott*!' and bobbed her head quickly in embarrassment.

Beyond the village they passed a creamy ox bearing panniers of bright pale wood, and the goats skipped past on their brittle legs, bleating an incomprehensible derision at the slow soiled beast, but Doris loved its soft, stupid eyes and the heavy slither of its muscles; and when the man with the whip gave them surprised greeting she did not mind that he stared at her open-mouthed.

'*Grüss Gott*!' she replied, clear and singing as a bird.

'Hey-hey-hey!' Josef called sharply to the goats, and ran to edge them away from the high red bank the river made as it rushed beyond the village and tumbled down the rocks in a cataract.

In action the tension went out of him. He moved with queer, quick little hops, sideways, flailing his arms, rebuking the animals with little soft cooing sounds of contempt. But when the goats were back on the path the constraint fell upon him again, and they were silent as they crossed the river. The bridge was old and wooden, with a sloping roof where the reflection of moving water slid in the cool and resin-smelling shade. The goats' hoofs rapped across the old warped planking, and their rumps flicked slyly, all dappled over with greenish light. Beside her she could hear the man's breathing, soft and quick, held in; and the green light coming up under the harsh planes of his averted face made the face seem to float beside her: a drowned face crowned with hair as heavy and green as saturated weed.

In the aching-bright sunlight that opened out beyond the bridge's tunnel Christ waited, hanging sad and heavy in a wayside shrine, crudely carved and painted an improbable blue. All about the naked feet there were small yellow explosions of buttercups, and tiny puffs of forget-me-nots among the piled cones of red and yellow maize. Josef bent his knee and crossed himself quickly, and his mouth moved as he passed the shrine. The goats leapt, tossing their shell-like horns, and bounded away up the hill.

'They go,' he said flatly. 'They know their way now.'

Disappointment pierced Doris so sharply that the sunlight blurred and shivered across her eyes. Then Josef's face formed again, all the sharp planes of it curiously gilded, as though the peculiar desperation of his expression was somehow fixed immutably, and she heard his voice grating on a harsh note of urgency:

'It is a small climb. But the view. . . .'

'I'm very strong really,' she said, in a strained, foolish little voice, and he stared at her with a cautious wonder, his face suddenly loose and uncontrolled, as though he might laugh, or burst into tears. But he only nodded, and said, 'If you grow tired you will tell me.'

For an hour they climbed, skirting the soft meadows and the top-heavy houses that hugged the hills. A farmer in a woollen cape greeted them, leaning on a neat post-and-rail fence and watching after them until they had rounded the shoulder of the hill. A woman with a bright red kerchief waved to them from a field, two children called to them from a doorway.

Always he walked a little ahead, his shoulders bowed and head lowered. She could see the separate hairs curling up coarse and thick between the tense cords of his neck, and a purplish birthmark moving with the delicate movement of his dark knee above the thick white sock. He did not turn to look at her, but she knew that he felt her there, scrambling and stumbling behind him, and the knowledge filled her with a fierce expectancy, more violent than anything she had ever known.

Before them, high on the curve of the hill, the goats paused, heraldic on a grey boulder, before they plunged away into a larch covert.

'It is not far now,' he said roughly, waiting for her. 'We go through the wood.' All words seemed difficult for him, as though verbal communication laid some intolerable strain on his inner sensitivity, and he used his English crudely, with a sort of anger against it. But she was dishevelled and panting and stumbling now with difficulty in her cheap, elaborate little walking shoes and his eyes had compassion for her. 'You are tired,' he said, but she shook her head dumbly and followed him still.

The larches ran deep across the hillside, stirring with cool air, and gentians starred the carpet of needles beneath their feet. There was no sound of their footfalls, and she felt the torment releasing in him. He was smooth and indistinct before her, his movement fluid and blended with the air; but she was a feverish glitter in the calm wood, diamond-hard in the diffuseness, and she stumbled through the gentians in a sudden agony of impatience.

The trees thinned out to a broad grassy terrace, swinging with the sound of many little bells, and the two goats bounded over the shoulders of the ridge to join the main flock.

Josef, unwary still with the spell of the wood, turned and

looked down into the deep sunny bowl of the valley. 'Look now,' he said gently, and his spread hands curved, offering it all to her like a mystical cup.

Doris did not hear him. She was staring above the terrace, where grey rocks blurred into the edge of the pine forest, smudged blue-black under the snowline. Beyond and above, receding from her, yet so near, so pure and dazzling and strong, the mountain surged upward to its glittering crest.

'Wild Emperor!' It was a soundless cry, although her thin throat moved and her mouth hung over the name. Her blue eyes filled and brimmed with the mountain.

He turned and saw her, and suddenly began to tremble; plucked at her sleeve and spoke quickly, his voice loud and strained in an incongruous overtone of cajolery. 'Look, look, Frau Piggott! Look now! Over there the *Gasthof*. See the angel shining. So gold and bright it is! The village, see? Like houses for dolls . . . a toy cow, there in the farm meadow . . . the church so little . . . so very little . . . shining . . . look, Frau Piggott . . . down . . . the river, the bridge there, the mill . . . down!'

His face was bent to her, blotting out the mountain; his fingers had gripped her shoulder, hurting. She looked at him, uncomprehending, seeing the minute shining drops of moisture springing and trembling on the dark grained skin, and her own slack mouth and startled eyes reflected doubly like pictures on black glass.

'But why are you afraid?' she asked.

His fingers releasing her shoulder left five points of pressure throbbing. She rubbed at the place, childishly, her eyes blurred with tears. She grieved for the man's dark haunted face, yet behind him the mountain soared, clean and white and strong.

'I . . . I have tried . . . .' Josef began, but the words dropped bleak and desolate between them, without meaning. And then he turned to her wildly and raised his fist and began to beat it against a lichened boulder as if it was her soft sad face he would batter into understanding. '*I have tried*!' he shouted, and the goats set up a terrified bleating, and the air jangled with their bells as they rushed wildly up the hill.

'There,' Doris said forlornly through her tears. 'It's all right. It's quite all right. It doesn't matter really.' She turned her back to the mountain and leant beside him against the cool rough stone, staring blindly down into the beauty of the valley. After a time he lifted his head from his arms and spoke to her.

'You do not know how it is,' he said. 'In a prison they make a man unsure . . . that is it, unsure.' The muscles jerked angrily under the high brown ridges of his cheeks. He slapped his bruised hand softly against the boulder as he spoke. 'When a man is unsure,' he said, 'fear comes.'

'There,' Doris said. 'There.' She touched his hand timidly. It was dry and hard and hot, with a curious silkiness, like fur, where the fine black hair downed his wrist. Her fingers continued to stroke his hand, automatically, and after a time she said, 'Harry's mother is always polishing the furniture. Polishing. Polishing. It's new, all of it. She looks at me and sniffs. She polishes the soot off. The fog gets in.' And then she said, 'The bed has a pink satin cover, and there's a doll on it that Harry gave me. Harry gives me presents. Every time . . . .'

Josef's hand closed over hers, quickly, pressing her palm down against the cool damp mosses on the boulder. They stood together quietly, and the thin boundless air eddied about them, moving with the bells, thick with the smell of goats and pines. And as if she stroked its flanks, Doris felt the mountain behind her, rising inevitably out of the space and clarity and pungency, soaring up without impediment.

Gently, filled with sorrow for him, she withdrew her hand, 'There,' she said, straightening with sudden decision. 'I've got to climb that mountain,' she said. 'Somehow I've got to.'

He was very still beside her, carved dark against the grey boulder. Only his eyes seemed alive, watching her, cautiously moving from the soft set face down to the elaborate fringes and tassels of her useless little shoes. He looked at her shoes for a long time.

REQUIEM MASS

*

by George Johnston

How strange to think of him lying there in that big high room. Such a bland room, with the pale light coming in from the east and softened by the unsuspected presence of the Thames just behind the wall. The perfect painter's light, he used to say; and say it with that comical grimace of his, as if to derogate his own reputation as an artist.

From the great windows of the studio one could see only the mellow wall and against it the sketchy pattern which a winter's withering had created from frail vines and creepers.

The tracery of the bare twigs seemed something almost contrived behind the solidity of the nudes, cast in concrete, half life-size; the models he had had, twelve of them ranged around the walls.

It was an old house, early Regency and perfect in its fashion, barely a hop-skip-and-a-jump from Cheyne Walk. It had been severely damaged by blast in one of the air-raids of 1941, enabling him, in the rebuilding, to put in the vast east windows, and to include the minstrel gallery and the wall upon which he had painted his meticulous imitation of a Gobelin tapestry.

Although the house was so near the river the only view of it was, incongruously, from the window of an upstairs toilet; from there the aspect was as lovely as it was unexpected – a slow barge sliding on the grey shine of the stream and, beyond it,

magical in the mist, the pale gigantic chimney-stacks of Battersea
Power Station.

I remember the toilet with some clarity because it was while I
was there on my first visit to his house — noting with a certain
surprise the presence of both a *bidet* and a shower recess in place
of the more normal apparatus of an Englishman's bathroom —
that he added considerably to my amazement by bursting into the
room without a by-your-leave, flinging wide the window, and
excitedly commanding me 'Look!' It was, admittedly, worth
looking at. Over the river, air and water had blended into a sheen
of damp and luminous silver, with the orange balloon of the sun
churning in the smoke from the power station's chimney.

'Had the Persians possessed *that*,' he cried, jabbing his finger
toward the power station, 'the cult of Mithras would have been
kept alive at least a millennium longer!'

Yes, I suppose he was a snob of sorts; yet he was the most
utterly gregarious of men. He would confess vociferously, even
eagerly, to snobbery, yet never really appear to practise it. To
every visitor he would point out delightedly the words of Horace
carved into the lintel of the entrance, *Odi profanum vulgus et arceo*,
and although he was for ever publicly wondering who had set the
words there — he even invented, as a peg for this responsibility,
a previous tenant, a misanthrope of the 1850s whom he called
Doctor Ramshaw — I suspect the truth was that he had carved
the words there himself. He was like that. He had a multitude of
small deceits.

It *is* strange to think of him lying there in that room he loved
so much, that room which brought all his deceits alive, and
warmed them, and made them truths of a sort — to him.

I can think of him lying there, but it is an abstract thought, for
I cannot *picture* him. The picture is insistently alive: of him seated
upon his high wooden stool, his small slippered feet swinging a
good six inches above the polished floor, his smock tucked beneath
him, his thin elbows on the tall Victorian bookkeeper's desk

where he would brood over his sketches and his music manuscripts and his notes, his pointed chin pressed into the inverted arch of his hands.

I can see him thoughtfully following the score of one of Scarlatti's harpsichord sonatas or that last *Lachrimosa* of Mozart's while the big phonograph played in the corner (he had a Bechstein, but to my knowledge it was never played); or roughing out a sketch with the sepia ink and the reed pens which he cut himself and which so often served as an excuse for some impulsive jaunt to France in search of the right bamboos.

For all the opulent improbability of its decor, the studio room had considerable charm and beauty. It suited him perfectly. Behind his high desk was a large ornate mirror – early 16th-century Italian, and genuine – set into a gilt portico and hung with a blue drape. The lower edge of the glass was flush with the floor so that the mirror presented the illusion of being a handsome doorway leading into an adjacent salon, equally large, equally drenched in the pale light, equally cluttered with the spoils of twenty years of artistic plundering of the Continent.

On the walls were some of his own paintings – portraits and nudes of exotic women, Indians, West Africans, Jamaicans, Burmese; a number of *genre* studies improbably bright and luminous with the light of Provencal markets and Breton quaysides and Tuscan farms. The portraits were very good, the smaller works quite charming and skilful, all of them: a little *too* charming, possibly, for after seeing them a few times one was inclined to remember their vivid insincerity and quite forget the undoubted technical skill which had gone into their creation.

I remember how one would turn away from his paintings with a faint, guilty sense of relief; turn away to the crumbling stone figure of a 12th-century saint pillaged from some abandoned Romanesque church along the Dordogne, to a superb primitive Virgin of cracked wood with flecks of polychrome still lodged like faded scraps of cloth in the crevices, to the big Italian chest with its cumbersome gilding and cracked wood panels of allegorical subjects painted rather poorly by some studio hack of 17th-century Venice but now given a quality of great, if insouciant charm, like a mosaic from Pompeii or one of the frescoes in the Etruscan tombs.

It was where I had first met him, grubbing among Etruscan tombs at the foot of the cliff beneath the walls of Orvieto.

I still have a reference to his appearance then as his small figure came, quick and eager, along the narrow path, with the white-foaming *petit-angelo* and the spiky asphodel standing high above his head on either hand. There was a quicksilver mobility about him, and as he hurried toward me I had the curious thought that he was half-plant, half-faun – not human at all. In his agitation the great mane of silky white hair tossed above his narrow face like thistledown, as if at any moment he might burst with a puff and scatter tiny white seed-darts into the air all about him.

He was then not quite sixty. So that Erica, who was exactly half his age, would have been nearly thirty.

It was impossible not to have talked to him, inevitable that after a cursory survey of the dank tombs with their cobwebs and wet green slabs I should walk back to the town with him. He talked incessantly and engagingly: of Signorelli's frescoes; of the enchanting manner in which the Umbrian weeds had grown to the very Cathedral door, and through the mosaics and all over Maitani's peerless façade; of Etruscan funerary rites; of the holy bloodstains on the cloth in Vieri's golden shrine; of Sienese goldsmiths. He quoted d'Annunzio's opinion of Orvieto, and Dante's; and offered his own opinions on Umbrian food, on Italian sports cars and on a bicycle race which had taken most of the town's population out on to the plain. But for the astonishing breadth and depth of his knowledge, and the whimsical manner in which he could switch from a cynical iconoclasm to the most devoted adoration almost in the space of a single sentence, one might have dismissed his conversation as the sheerest prattle. As it was, I found it enchanting.

Indeed it was for fear of losing his companionship that I suggested refreshment – 'A bottle of wine, an *espresso*?' – at an iron table outside a rather grubby hotel on the via Garibaldi.

'Yes.' He accepted, smiling. 'But what? The "sweet white wine of Orvieto" – which any sensible palate will abhor – or the Montefiascone which is dangerous at this time of day? In Italy the choice is invariably an unhappy one.'

I laughed. 'You seem to know the ropes far better than I do. The decision will have to be yours.'

'Then the white,' he said cheerfully. 'Distress is usually only temporary; peril may be permanent.'

We must have been drinking and talking an hour or more before Erica came.

She was wearing white linen and when I first caught sight of her she was sauntering in our direction down the almost empty street, swinging a big Florentine leather bag negligently from one hand. From a distance she did not look particularly beautiful, although she walked well and there was something about her that compelled attention. Orvieto, you must understand, is a curious town, high on its great rock against the rain-white Umbrian sky, and even when the most of its population has not been spirited away by a bicycle race its most striking characteristic is one of emptiness and silence: a brooding quality as if none dare even whisper lest he evoke again the ancient darkness, sinister and bloody and tragic. On this day, with the town shuttered and practically abandoned, the quiet emptiness of everything seemed to flow into and to be utterly contained by the slender figure in white that came slowly toward us.

I saw Halliday's eyes rest thoughtfully for a moment upon her, but he was talking of a wine he had tasted in the Medoc and, after only the briefest pause, he continued: '...and the bouquet magically faint, rather like the half-memory of some fragment of sweet music heard long ago. It was a long time before I could bring myself to sip it. And then . . . .'

I was scarcely listening to him, for to my astonishment I saw that the woman had come up to us and was standing beside the table looking down at him with a faint smile at her mouth. His eyes met hers quickly, without warmth or even recognition, and turned back to mine. 'And then,' he continued, 'I think I knew what the gods once drank on Olympus. Yet *more* than nectar – the very blood of Dionysius!'

Not until then, not until he had finished his sentence, did he acknowledge her presence.

'Darling,' he said, rising. 'Pleasant walk?' And then he introduced us: 'This is my wife, Erica Halliday.'

Her hand was small and cool, her smile the same.

'Why not cut along to your room, dear, and freshen up?' he suggested quickly. 'Our talk, I'm afraid, would bore you stiff, but we shan't be much longer. You must be exhausted in this heat.'

'Perhaps Mrs Halliday would care to join us in a drink,' I said, and then, realising how desperately I wished to make amends for his earlier discourtesy – if discourtesy it was – I flushed slightly, and quickly added: 'In spite of your husband's condemnation, I confess I find the Orvieto very pleasant indeed.'

Again she looked at him with the same queer, faint smile, but when she turned to me the smile seemed warmer. Or did I imagine it? 'Thank you,' she said quietly. 'If you will forgive me, I think I shall go to my room. I have a slight headache. This heat! If the rain would only come up from the valley.'

She had hardly gone from us before Halliday turned to me again. 'One sip, my dear Burton, and I tell you I understood everything. *Everything!* The Mysteries . . . Pan . . . the maenads . . . *everything.*'

His wife did not return, and after a time I left him. They were not at the hotel next morning – the porter explained that they had made a very early start – and I strolled up to the Duomo. It was interesting to discover that I had quite new thoughts about Maitani's façade since I had heard Halliday talk about it. After lunch I drove on to Perugia.

The Umbrian landscape, all brown and olive under a pale, steamy sky, possessed a placidity that invited one's thoughts to wander; but it was Erica Halliday, whom I had not seen for more than a few minutes, and not her loquacious, erudite husband, who occupied my mind.

I could no longer remember whether she was tall or short, attractive or commonplace. What I could remember was her almost startling air of *quietness*: a sort of timeless quietness, a passive withdrawal into environment. 'Landscape with figure,' I muttered to myself. 'Street scene with figure of young woman.' I felt, absurdly, that if I were to come again to the via Garibaldi a thousand years hence I would still find her there, aimless before the shuttered shops, the leather bag twirling slowly from her fingers.

Possibly I would never have seen them again had I not come across an amusing letter in *The Times* almost a year later. It was an erudite and extremely witty criticism of the cleaning of some Rubens or other in the National Gallery, and it was signed their obedient servant Sefton Halliday, ARA.

The address was given and, on an impulse, I sat down and scribbled a short note to him, expressing my amusement and recalling our brief meeting at Orvieto.

Two days later I was summoned to the telephone.

'Mr Burton?' It was a woman's voice, very quiet. 'This is Erica Halliday. We were so pleased to receive your letter....' There was a longish pause, as if she were wondering what the devil to say next.

'Not as pleased as I was to read your husband's,' I put in helpfully. 'I was so amused, I could not resist dropping him some little line of appreciation. Naturally, I hadn't thought he would remember Orvieto. After all – '

'Of course we remembered. Last month, when your book appeared, we read some notices. We had intended to write. Yes, we remembered having met you.' Another long pause. 'I am afraid my husband is not at home today, but he asked me to ring . . . .' (I could hear his voice faint in the background, but still sharp and insistent: 'Tell him seven-thirty – absolutely informal.') 'We are having some friends along to dinner on Friday. Quite informal. If you were not doing anything we were hoping . . . .'

'I'd be delighted.'

'Come about seven-thirty,' she said.

I found myself looking toward the occasion with some pleasure. I had been so much out of England in the few preceding years that almost all my social contacts had lapsed, and my visits to London never lasted longer than the necessity for completing what research I had to do at the British Museum or the Institute. It is the dreary mud of England, I think, as much as the dreary monoliths, that drives the archaeologist so hungrily to distant deserts; but it is perhaps the deserts which, recurrently, make the Englishman savour with especial relish the prospect of a Chelsea dinner party. I was not disappointed. I enjoyed my first visit to the Hallidays as much as I had enjoyed anything in years.

He was a delightful host and the quality of his food and wine illustrated clearly that his conversation at Orvieto had not been idle. There were only five other guests: a BBC man and a young sculptor predisposed toward a moody intensity that seemed to have not the slightest effect on anybody. The wife of the first was a chatterbox blonde who reminded me of one of those golden clockwork birds made to amuse despotic Chinese emperors; the sculptor's wife appeared to have abandoned herself to the complacent detachment of her advanced state of pregnancy. The two men paid no attention whatsoever to the women – the sculptor out of pure moroseness, the BBC man because of a twittering anxiety to immerse himself in the conversation, like a sparrow in a birdbath – so that it was quite late in the evening before I could be sure which woman was the wife of which man. The other guest was a quiet, middle-aged textile manufacturer from the Midlands who seemed to accept his improbability with great good nature. Halliday, I gathered, had done portraits of his wife and children.

Halliday, basking in the effulgence of excellent wine and food and stimulating company, was in top form. Whether he really knew the subject or whether, knowing my field of interest, he had gone to the trouble of briefing himself, I shall never really know; the fact remains that talking to him on archaeology was uncannily like talking to a textbook. He was, at the same time, an excellent listener, warming and encouraging one with his obvious interest. Nevertheless I can still recapture my astonishment when he discussed the curious tombs of Malta and the Hal Tarxien temples, for I have never known any person outside the very limited field of experts in this rather neglected subject to have so much knowledge, nor any one of them to display so much originality in his hypotheses.

It was not until I was putting on my overcoat that I really had an opportunity of talking to his wife. He had gone outside to pack the two men and the wives into the BBC man's car.

'It was really very nice of you to come,' she said evenly. 'It has been fascinating for all of us.' She paused. 'I wanted to tell you,' she added, 'that I admired your book very much indeed.'

'Thank you,' I said.

'I thought Sefton would have told you. He liked it too. Enormously.' She smiled faintly. 'I think he got carried away by the conversation. Or perhaps he wished *me* to tell you how much we enjoyed it. Being about Greece, your book, I mean. I am Greek, you see.'

'Really?' Loking at her, I had a quick, curious memory of the ruined Temple of Poseidon on that lonely headland at Cape Sunium, such a grave temple, so quiet and pale and *alone*. 'I had no idea....'

'Actually, I was born in Cyprus, but when — '

'Well, well!' It was her husband, back from the front door, rubbing his hands together gleefully. 'I say, Burton, I'm afraid you *are* the success of the evening. Charrington swears he'll have you on the Third Programme within a week.'

Going home I found myself musing upon how curious it was that Halliday, knowing my interest in Greece, had never told me that his wife was Greek.

There was some new digging to be done west of Epidaurus that spring, and I sailed for Athens the following week. I saw nothing of them, consequently, until the autumn, although quite fortuitously I was able to piece a little more together as a result of a chance encounter in Athens.

I had gone to the capital to attend a special lecture series which had been organised by the British Council, and it was there that I met Boyce-Garston. He buttonholed me very early in the evening to seek my advice, as to whether his projected cycle of the *Theban Plays* would be more appropriate in the theatrical setting of Delphi or beneath the sinister and more symbolic walls of Mycenae. I assured him that both were extremely remote and draughty and certain to be intimidating to all but the most hardy classicists.

'To say nothing,' I added with a smile, 'of being hideously uncomfortable.'

'I really don't feel comfort is that important when there is a thing to do,' he said tiredly, and I could not but agree with him.

It must have been I who brought Halliday into the conversation, for I remember Boyce-Garston glancing up at me quickly and saying, 'You know Halliday then?'

'Only slightly.'

'Ah,' he said, and nodded thoughtfully, as if he had seen and understood some weighty implication behind my simple statement. 'I shall never forgive Halliday,' he went on, 'for having taken Erica away.'

'Erica?'

'Erica Kiranos. His wife. You know her, of course.'

'Not well, I'm afraid.'

'But you saw her act? No? *Never?*' He stared at me for a moment, then shook his head with a quick air of wildness. 'Her Medea! Young for a Medea admittedly, but really quite superb. And that simply *delicious* Lysistrata of hers.' He sighed.

'I'm afraid I had not even known she was an actress,' I murmured. 'I had . . . .'

'Not *known*?' I could tell from his expression that any advice I had been able to give him about the setting for the *Theban Plays* had been quite discounted. 'Erica Kiranos? But, my dear chap, six years ago half London was raving about her.'

'I must have been out of London at the time,' I said apologetically. 'Yes, of course — that would have been the time of the Anatolian expedition. I am always guilty, I'm afraid, of not keeping in touch when I'm away.'

'Quite,' he said forgivingly.

'Does she still act, then?'

'Heavens, no! That's the absolute hell of it. Why she should have married Halliday in the first place — a not terribly exciting artist, by the way, and old enough to be her father — is a complete mystery. But she did. She did. Deserted the stage completely, dedicated to the role of dutiful wife, motherhood, all that sort of nonsense — and simply disappeared into an abyss of blank obscurity. Absolutely tragic!'

'Motherhood, you say? But surely there is no family?'

'Not a sausage, old man. It *was* her intention, but one gathers *he* is not fond of children. Consequently she got nothing at all out of it except the obscurity. Often happens that way, you know. She is, naturally, utterly miserable with him, but then she has that curious Greek thing of loyalty. You know how the Greek women are with their men.'

'But I dined with them a week before I left London,' I expostulated. 'I had the impression they were perfectly happy.'

He shrugged. 'As I was saying, she is by nature an astonishingly good actress. That, and this Greek trait of hers ... well ....' He smiled tiredly and took himself off, evidently to seek out somebody of sounder intelligence to advise him on his *Theban Plays*.

That summer was tedious and almost completely unproductive and we abandoned the site near Epidaurus with no particular regrets at the end of August. I had some cataloguing to do in Athens and it was late October before I returned to London. It was cold and foggy, with the fallen leaves making a yellow paste across the pavements. The sun had taken on its inflamed winter shape and colour, and briefly each day would seem to trundle along not much higher than the level of the Thames, misshapen and with a sullen smoulder, like a once-bright ball of fire that has been tossed about too often.

Small paragraphs had appeared in both *The Times* and the *Telegraph* about my return, and that evening my telephone rang. It was Halliday. Could I take a taxi and come over for dinner? Just the two of them. There was so much they wanted to hear from me ....

It was from this point that an acquaintanceship as casual and superficial as anything sprung from the passing propinquity of a steamer passage developed into something close approaching intimacy.

It was on this night that he first played the *Requiem Mass*, the work that Mozart never finished. The lights were out in the big studio; only the flickering firelight and the dull glow of the valves in the radiogram and the grey-purple darkness through the big windows and the occasional red glow of the cigarette like a hole in the shadows of the sofa where Erica was curled up. He was perched on his high stool, curiously imp-like with the firelight accentuating his pointed features and glittering eyes and the dark shadows dancing above him.

The speaker was set into the wall just above the cracked wooden Virgin in the corner, but gradually the unearthly voices of the choir seemed to move out into the room, swirling around us, drifting and darting with the shadows, voices dark as hell and bright as fire. It was all a little eerie.

Then suddenly Halliday spoke. 'Look at Erica,' he said, with a sort of suppressed glee. 'She will be weeping. She always weeps.' He chuckled softly.

A log moved in the fire, and spat sparks. And in the sudden brightness I saw her face. She *was* weeping, quite silently, quite tragically, her jaw slack, her mouth open, her fingers trembling at her temples. In that brief moment of light it was a sight quite piteous, completely horrifying. And then the log slowly rolled over and turned to us its blackened side, and in the plunge of darkness she left the room without a sound.

When the music had ended, Halliday switched on the lights and turned to me with an amused laugh.

'She's always the same,' he chuckled. 'I can honestly say I've never known her *not* to weep. What is it? Something psychic possibly? Some ultrasonic sensibility, something *she* hears that is quite beyond the range of our faculties?'

'Or just emotion,' I suggested. 'After all, it *is* extraordinarily moving music.'

'I think something more, Burton.' He grinned. 'It fascinates me.'

She returned to the room a little later, with the coffee, as if nothing had happened.

I said to her, 'By the way, it betrays my ignorance, but it was not until quite recently, in Athens as a matter of fact, that I learnt you had been on the stage.'

'My dear Burton, it *does* betray your ignorance,' Halliday laughed. 'Why, she was the toast of the town – of Chelsea, anyway, and Notting Hill Gate.' He turned to her. 'It was where I discovered you, wasn't it, darling? Rehearsing Webster, of all things! I ask you, Burton, can you imagine Erica playing the Duchess of Malfi, rampaging around the stage with knives and poison, up to her thighs in blood?'

I was about to say something, but he was laughing and she smiling at him, and then the talk went on to something else. But I think I began to realise then that Boyce-Garston's observation might not have been entirely off the mark.

I saw much of them both through that winter, and when spring came I accepted with eagerness an invitation to accompany them on a month's tour of the south of France. It had been a good many years since I had allowed myself a completely non-professional, carefree holiday, and I found the experience most stimulating. Part of this, I confess, derived from an interest in Erica, for I had grown to like her very much; but partly it was a more general thing – a sort of realisation that after years of dissecting the toppled columns and broken shards of dead civilisations it was a rare delight to find oneself so closely studying living humanity, in all its quick flux and with all its foibles.

It was the sort of journey where nothing is ever really planned, where one sets out with a vague general idea of where one wants to go and what one wants to see, but with a tacit willingness to surrender easily to digression. It was never until the evening that we knew whether we were to be pleased or frustrated. Erica accepted it all, good or bad, pleasure or privation, with an unruffled calm that sometimes seemed close to indifference. Halliday, who was very much the organiser, was more easily upset. He could be thrown into ecstasies by an excellent omelette or an unexpectedly good wine or the picture of some crumbling market-place seen from the window of his hotel room. He would as quickly lapse into sulky silence or become querulous or argumentative if the anticipated delights were withheld from him by the dourness of some surly *hotelier*, by drab surroundings, or a dreary table.

We must have been travelling in our staccato, impulsive manner for about ten days before it began to occur to me that there was a faint but undeniable flavour of hysteria about our progress.

Plotted on the roadmap, ours was an erratic course, full of yawings and veerings like a rudderless yacht – a chart, in fact, of Halliday's restless whims. Erica, having spent years at the Sorbonne, spoke faultless French. Mine was fair. His was excellent conversational French, but with an accent you could cut with a knife, and he had a mania for attempting the most impossible tricks with *patois*. When his listeners failed to understand him he would become furious. Yet it was he who did all the talking, made all the arrangements, conducted all the bargaining. Erica seldom bothered to talk the language at all, and indeed there were paradoxical moments when she would ask some question in English and he would interpret for her! Neither of them seemed to see anything odd in this.

As I was in their hands, and their guest – and enjoying myself enormously – I seldom offered suggestions. If I did so Halliday would accept them instantly and with great warmth, and make elaborate revisions of his own arrangements to fall in with my idea. Erica's suggestions, infrequently made, were always discounted quickly or disregarded altogether.

There were occasions, of course, when Halliday's command of the expedition would have wearying results. Once we travelled three hundred miles back to the Touraine simply because he had become involved in a dispute with a drink waiter about the quality of some particular vintage *Vouvray*. We devoted two whole days to a vain search for a bottle of *Pouilly-Fumé* because he had remembered drinking it on a visit to the Loire some years before. As the potential victim of these unpredictable and exhausting whims, I found myself becoming extremely guarded in after-dinner conversations, lest some innocent discussion of the Albigensian Heresy send us rocketing over the wicked black mountains to Albi itself!

I felt that I was gradually beginning to understand Erica's attitude of passive detachment, of apparent disinterestedness.

And then came that Sunday afternoon at Sarlat to show me how completely I had misunderstood it.

We had enjoyed an excellent lunch, and, sipping our cognac, it was very pleasant and restful in that wonderful market-place which might have seemed so completely a museum of medieval architecture but for the contemporary bustle of the people and the stalls.

We had been there about half an hour, almost stupefied by contentment, when Halliday suddenly gulped down his brandy, excused himself, and darted off, shouting back to us about some inquiry he must make. I watched him go, skipping through the crowd, and turned to Erica.

'Why on earth is Sefton always moving so fast?' I asked. 'Can he never relax?'

Erica's dark eyes concentrated on the pale polished tip of her finger, tracing monotonously round and round the rim of her glass. She said at last: 'He is like a child. He lives always on the surface of his life. And he must for ever move across it very quickly. I think he is afraid that if he pauses the weight of it will be too much, and the surface tension will break, and he will go down into deep parts.' She smiled a little then, and looked at me directly. 'In those deep parts, you see, he cannot swim.'

'I see,' I said, and lit a cigarette.

'And, of course, he hates me,' she went on quietly, as if it was an afterthought of little importance.

I looked at her sharply, but the faint smile was still at her mouth, and her finger went on tracing the same unending circle.

'Erica! What a monstrous suggestion!' I spoke as lightly as I could, although her words, taken with the expression in her eyes, had startled me considerably. Her sensitive, unpainted mouth was very pale and tight, and then she gave a queer little shrug as if to say, *Oh well, the cat's out of the bag now.*

'Listen, Brian,' she said, meeting me directly with those quiet eyes of hers, so dark and honest. '*Resents* may be a more polite word, but it isn't the word I mean. *Hate* may not be the right word either, but at least it is a cold, implacable word. And this is a cold, implacable thing he feels towards me – no, perhaps not *feels*, not yet, anyway. Suspects, rather.' She moistened her lips, and went on in a lower voice: 'That is why he must be for ever moving. He is safe, perhaps, while he only suspects, but he must not stop, not pause, for then he would have time to *know* it, and he would go down into the deep parts, the terrifying parts.' She smiled quickly at me then, and finished her drink. 'You wanted to know why he moves so fast,' she said.

'Oh, come now, Erica, this is – '

'I think it *is* true, Brian. I am certain it is why he is driven by this hunger, this fever to *do* things, to *know* things, this insatiable curiosity about places and people and things – to meet people, *new* people. To meet *you*. To him, Brian, you were a wonderful discovery, because you were two things – a new person and a new field of interest that would choke his mind with a whole fresh crop of facts and with so much thinking that there would be no room in it any longer for . . . for thought.'

'Are you sure you're not exaggerating all this just a little, Erica?' I said gently. 'After all, he is – '

'Of course I'm exaggerating.' She smiled and her cool fingers touched my hand for a moment. 'You're sweet to have been so tolerant. Forgive me, Brian. Too much French food, too much sunshine, too much cognac.' She laughed – that rare, brilliant laugh of hers that could transform her instantly into a woman of quite astonishing beauty.

78

Halliday was coming towards us, jostling through the crowd. Red-faced, panting, his eyes alight, he was shouting at us before he reached the table:

'Come on now! Drink them up! I've just heard of the most fantastic private museum out on the Montignac road, just up from Le Moustier – we must have driven right past the dashed place yesterday – and a simply heavenly pub in the valley. I've got the petrol in the car. So come on now!'

Back in London I found it not quite as easy as I had expected to push into the back of my mind that conversation with Erica. It would keep popping out so that sometimes I found myself watching them speculatively and reading more meaning into chance expressions and remarks than perhaps were even intended. Certainly Erica never referred again to that afternoon in Sarlat, and apart from an occasional uneasiness I continued to find them a charming couple. Yet occasionally ... occasionally I felt positive there was something slightly *wrong*, something off-key, as it were.

The Royal Academy's summer exhibition, for instance, a few months after our return from France. They had hung two of Halliday's portraits, neither of which I felt were up to his best standard. The notices, for the most part, either ignored the paintings altogether or dismissed them with a tepid phrase or two; one notice, however, was quite spiteful and it hurt Halliday deeply, having been written by a young man who had dined often at the house and whom Halliday had helped very considerably in his career. Halliday was characteristically jocular about it all.

'Well, that will jolly well teach me' – he grinned – 'to play indulgent father to an asp.'

'Be grateful,' I said lightly, 'that it was only a temporary paternity. At least this relieves you of further responsibility.'

He was shuffling around the papers on the bookkeeper's desk, but at this he slammed the inkwell down so forcibly that brown ink splashed across his sketches. He used a short and extremely unpleasant word.

'I suppose,' he said tartly, 'that remark was inspired by my poor barren wife. God almighty, Burton, I do abhor martyrs!' And then he looked across at me with a chuckle. 'I ask you, can you see Erica crooning little lullabies and wiping snotty noses?'

I think he was rather sorry about his outburst and vaguely apologetic. At dinner he was an absolute virtuoso, playing on words and ideas with such gaiety and skill that he enthralled me: by comparison, Erica's cool detachment seemed to lack responsiveness to an unreasonable degree.

You must not think that such outbursts happened often: they were, in fact, infrequent. Erica's conversation seldom touched a personal plane, and her husband had so many other things to talk about that he seldom spoke of his own relationship with her. But they had come to accept me as an intimate family friend. They were not quite so much on their guard. There were chance remarks, seeming to hang in air, lacking association with what had been said, what would be said; there were Halliday's occasional flashes of asperity.

Once, when a picture he was painting had failed to come easily, he complained to me, half-jokingly, that his creative force was waning. 'Comes of marrying a wealthy woman,' he said wryly. 'Too much soft padding round the spirit.'

On the following Sunday, walking in Kew Gardens with Erica, I said, 'Was Sefton poor when you first met him?'

She halted beneath the Lebanon cedar, looking up toward the lacquer red pagoda, and after an interval she turned and smiled at me.

'Oh, not out-at-elbows,' she said. 'But quite poor, yes.'

'Was his work better when he was poor than it is now?'

'I'm not sure. It might have been. Not enough, though, to support a policy of crusts and attics. Besides, he quite approves of his comforts, you know.'

'Yes.' I lit a cigarette. 'He was married before, wasn't he?'

'Yes.'

'What was she like?'

'I never knew her. I gather she was a good deal older than he, and ran up debts, and nagged, and kept his wings clipped. She had been his model when he was very young, still a student. He was frightfully ashamed of her – and of his children, too.

'They're all grown up now. Horrid people. They still ask for money sometimes. One of them, the eldest, was killed in the blitz. It was rather horrid. Somehow they found out about Sefton being his father, and they came around and wanted him to identify the body. He refused to go. He sent me instead.'

'But I understood you to say you were not acquainted with . . . with . . . .'

'Oh, I had met *this* one. Several times. He was the one who used to come for the money. Sefton would never see him.'

'Not even when he was dead?'

'He is terribly afraid of death. I suppose he felt that I was young – so much younger than he that I would not be afraid of death.'

'Everybody is a little afraid of death,' I said softly; and at this she turned with a quick, apologetic smile, and took my arm, and we walked together back toward the lake.

We did not speak. I was thinking of Halliday – and of how hard it must have been for him, growing old, and Erica so young and with most of her life still ahead of her. Was it that thought which had been in his mind the evening we drank claret together at Elvino's? He had suddenly made a comical grimace, self-mocking. 'Don't let anyone tell you about the compensations of age,' he had said. 'There aren't any. Only sciatica, and loose teeth, and time running out.'

That conversation in Kew Gardens was not the last talk I had with Erica, but it is the last that I can clearly recapture.

I was in my flat, reading a pamphlet before turning in, when it happened. The Hallidays' housekeeper had given my name to the police, and when they telephoned I dressed and drove across to Chelsea straight away.

There were two policemen waiting at the house, young men in mackintoshes, both very well-spoken and without any of the official detachment one might have expected. They were sympathetic, respectful, apologetic.

'Mostly a matter of formal identification, sir, and a few questions,' one of them said. 'There will be an inquest, but we shan't need to trouble you about that. We shall cause you as little inconvenience as possible, Mr Burton, but since you happen to be the most intimate acquaintance of the deceased couple . . . .'

'Of course.'

I remember being startled by the design of the mortuary chapel, by its square, white, almost Grecian simplicity. Both faces were curiously peaceful, Halliday's with the faintest trace of a smile at the pale mouth; Erica's grave and withdrawn, as detached from death as she had been from life.

After I had signed the papers we went back together to the house near the river.

They showed me where the bodies had been found – Halliday's huddled on the floor alongside the old bookkeeper's desk, Erica's in the bedroom near the big Breton chest. The two glasses that had contained the poisoned liquor had been taken away, but they pointed out to me where they had been discovered.

Their questions were the merest formalities. I told them what I could.

After they had gone I stayed behind to talk to the servants, to see if there was anything I could do to help them – a painful task, for they had been deeply attached to their employers – and then, for the last time, I went up into the big studio room.

All life had rushed out of it – later it would gradually trickle back again on the slow tides of memory – and it was as bereft of the passion and pulse of human affairs as any ruined temple or shattered statue of two thousand years ago.

I turned to leave, but looking across at the great pale windows as I switched off the light I saw a tiny glow smouldering at me from the corner of the room. The gramophone was still switched on. Even before I went across to look I knew that I would find Mozart's *Requiem Mass* on the turntable.

The inquest, held three days later, lasted only twelve minutes and brought in a finding, in both cases, of suicide while the balance of the mind was disturbed. The newspapers, in the popular prose of the day, told the story in five words, ACADEMICIAN-ACTRESS IN DEATH PACT, with two photographs – as grey and lifeless as the two dead faces – and a column of padding about their careers.

The world, I suppose, very quickly forgot Sefton and Erica Halliday.

But sometimes I still wonder which of them was the murderer. Obviously it was not a suicide pact. They had long since lost the sense of oneness, and nothing but that sense could have carried them through an undertaking so desperately mutual. Moreover they would have died together, in the same room – and they would not have played that record.

It was murder then – but by whom? And why?

Did he play the *Mass*, and Erica *not* weep? Or did he find, for some reason, her weeping something that no longer could be borne? Did he suddenly discover how alone he was, how alone he had been for all these years? Did his goading finally succeed in crashing to the earth that white, marble-like wall of Grecian reserve?

My mind keeps coming back to it, turning over, reconstructing, imagining, desperately trying to prove that it was Halliday. I am sure that it was Halliday, that it was he who poisoned her and then similarly destroyed himself. He was afraid of death, yes, but he was afraid of loneliness more. And in that quiet, beautiful room he loved so much I feel that he must have suddenly found himself alone for the first time, quite alone.

Erica could not have done it. We never spoke of it, but I am sure – as sure as I am of anything – that she was aware of my love for her. She would have known that she had something to live for.

But Halliday? Halliday had nothing, not anything at all, once reality moved into that room swirling with the spirit voices of the choir.

Now it is done. The house has been sold long since. The fragile cloche that Halliday built to protect his life from the dark, powerful forces that beset it has been destroyed to make room for some new cloche for some other life, equally piteous, equally vulnerable.

It all goes on, and sometimes it seems that only the fictitious Doctor Ramshaw retains reality.

And I – I who for so long was such a close observer of it all, I who for so many years had known loneliness and enjoyed it – have come at last to realise what it means to be alone.

THE SMALL ANIMUS

*

by *Charmian Clift*

We had not been living on the small Greek island of Kalymnos for more than a few weeks when the children began to be importunate – particularly Shane, who adds a refined female cunning to a child's natural capacity for the unwearied nagging of its distracted elders.

'In London you said ... you *promised* ....'

'If children don't keep a promise they aren't true ... they're something *awful*. But grown-ups don't have to, do they, mummy?' Shane's eyes were about as guileless as those of a Borgia dining out with the House of Sforza.

'Of course they have to. But ....'

'Well then, you *said*!'

'You *promised*!'

That night George, conceding defeat, took up the matter with Tony, a happy storekeeper who returned some years ago from America to his beloved native island bringing with him an intact soul, a small pension, an obsession with sanitation that borders on fanaticism, and an overwhelming passion for the English language (or, more correctly, those words of the English language that have more than three or four syllables) which he uses ironically to express his detestation of the English race.

'Listen now, Tony,' George said anxiously, 'we've promised the kids that we will find some sort of pet for them. When we were in London we said they could have one. You know, some sort of – '

'Them kids!' Tony rose to his feet, raised his cloth cap, and motioned for silence with the copper retzina beaker. 'Mr George and Mrs Charmian! When I confront certain elements . . . .'

This is Tony's invariable opening for what is inevitably a long, tortuous and utterly incomprehensible harangue, twisting its way to the final impassioned peroration on the iniquities of the British rule in Cyprus. By the time he got to Cyprus this night we were two beakers of retzina ahead and a bit discouraged about everything, including Cyprus. The rest of the clientele of the big taverna of Tasos Zordos – the sponge-divers and fishermen and labourers – looked pretty discouraged too; but then they couldn't follow even the single-syllable words, since Tony in all the passion of oratory had spoken in English. It was quite some time after he had sat down again, flushed and puffing with the pride of accomplishment, before anyone spoke, and then George said warily:

'That's fine, Tony. I understand your sentiments. But about the children, and that – '

'The children?' Tony studied him blankly. 'What have the children got to do with . . . with . . . . What is that goddam word now? Just now I *used* it! With . . . kids ain't concerned with . . . with *imperialism*!' He beamed. 'That's it! Imperialism! You know, Mr George, when I confront certain elements – '

'Yes, Tony, that's fine. Just fine. But these children of ours have asked for a pet. A small animal of some sort.'

'A small animus!' He shook his head hopelessly, his eyes dazed. 'What do you know now?' he said wonderingly. 'Kids is crazy elements. What do they go around wanting *that* for? Ain't they got this climate? Ain't they got a panorama Rockefeller couldn't buy?'

'An *animal*, Tony. A small animal. You know how children

86

are. A little dog, or a little cat of their own to look after —
some sort of animal.'

Comprehension lighted Tony's plump face with the mysterious joy of a child listening to a sea-shell.

'Ah, a small *animus*! Woof-woof-woof! Miaow-miaow!' He
slapped his thigh delightedly and again banged for silence.
'Listen here, you fellers, all of you. Petros, Anastasis, Dimitri,
Leonidas, Mikailis, listen you now. The Australian children
require the animus, creatures that are small and alive. You fetch
them now. Tomorrow you bring them to the house of our
friends. You understand what I mean? Small ones.' All the soft
brown eyes under the black cloth caps regarded us earnestly, and
with a little wonder.

'Only one animal, Tony,' George said hurriedly. 'One will do
beautifully.'

'Poof!' said Tony. 'These fellers bring you plenty. Don't you
worry no more now.' He shook his head admiringly. 'Them
kids of yours is the craziest element. Why,' he said, 'this town is
full of animus!'

'Yes,' George said bleakly, looking pale suddenly with the
realisation of what we had done. 'I know.'

They began to come at dawn, when the mountains were
washed rose-pink and the steep zigzag trail to Vathy looked like
a decorative motif scrawled on. The cubes of the houses were still
dark, with just a faint shelly gleam to them, and from the window
we could see the *Andros* — the passenger boat to Rhodes —
at anchor out beyond the sponge-boats, lit up in the darkness like
a department store at Christmas.

The children were awakened by the first thuds on the street
door, and before we could stop them they were hurtling down
the stairs. By the time we had scrambled out and fumbled for
candle and matches, the bolt was drawn, and they were squealing
upstairs again, towing behind them a polite and grinning young

sponge-diver, who rather sheepishly produced from his pocket a scraggy, bulging-eyed black kitten. It hung in his bleeding hand for a second before it bounded to the floor and scuttled into the kitchen with Martin and Shane in rapturous pursuit.

'Well,' said George, after we had thanked the young man and dabbed some Dettol on his wounds, 'at least it wasn't a donkey. Or a goat.'

'You wait,' I said. Down beneath the dark salt-trees beside the line of shuttered coffee-houses I could just make out the lean shape of Manolis the *raptis*. He was walking very carefully and holding well away from his body a large and heaving sack. Behind him, skipping around the white-painted tree boles on joyful young feet, was Vassilis the cigarette boy, and there was certainly something else on his wooden tray besides cigarettes. Something that wriggled.

'*Mum*!' Martin wailed from the kitchen. 'The kitten's up the chimney. And it's all *oily*!' Suppressed giggles from Shane, pattering back in her pyjamas. 'I think it's *done something* in the oil can.'

'Never mind about that,' George said shortly. 'Just you get downstairs again as fast as you can and bolt that door.'

Too late. It was nearly midday before we got the door bolted, and by that time it seemed that half the inhabitants of the island had come and gone, albeit with some bewilderment, having made their small presentations to the Australian children. They had come singly and in groups of two or three, the tall men with the fierce black moustaches and the shy brown eyes, and they had come with sacks and bulging pockets and baskets covered with clean checked cloths. George was ashen. Even the frenzied rapture of the children had staled: they walked warily, with their mouths open like cretins, and were inclined to cling to each other.

Apart from the kitten up the chimney – where it stayed

for a whole day until smoked out – there were seven others hissing and spitting from every dark corner and beneath all the beds. Not Listen-with Mother kittens either: these were the torn-eared, raw-boned, fanged and clawed children of their alley parents, and they weren't having any truck with friendly advances.

On the balcony a fierce red-eyed duck stomped backwards and forwards, hurling imprecations at the interested crowd assembled on the waterfront below; and in the kitchen our household help, Sevasti, clucked away in disapproving counterpoint to the despairing clucking of the trussed red hen lurching around the stone floor. Under George's writing desk two mangy little dogs shivered in cowed company, terrified, no doubt, of the swoops and sickening thuds of the three panic-stricken sparrows that just would not fly out of the open window. And in the centre of it all a very small white rabbit with long black ears sat imperturbably in a soup plate, munching on a cabbage leaf.

There was something awfully charming about that little rabbit. If the other spitting, clawing, furred and feathered monsters were straight from Bosch, the rabbit was the purest Disney.

Even at the awful climax of the nightmare, when George was hauling cats and dogs out from beneath the beds and the children were shrieking woe and Sevasti was grimly slaughtering the duck and the hen in the kitchen, the rabbit retained its composure, its boulevard air of *savoir-faire*. It was as if it possessed some inner certainty that it would survive the debacle, and could afford to devote its attention to the delicate task of pulling away the outer leaves of the cabbage to reach the succulent heart.

'That all them fellers brought you – just that one small animus?' Tony asked that night. Expertly, he picked up the little rabbit by the ears and jiggled it round a bit. There was a long string of lettuce hanging from its front teeth, and even dangling in mid-air the lettuce kept ascending and disappearing at the same steady rate. 'He's okay,' Tony said judicially. 'You keep him a bit, feed him up nice, he'll make a kilo maybe. A little butter . . . a few onions . . . .'

We had no intention of eating him, I said in what was meant to be a firm voice but was still rather a subdued tone because of the day's events. He was to be the children's pet.

He was a nice little pet, too. I had never had any particular feeling about rabbits before. Australians are not normally reared in the Flopsy Bunny tradition. Rabbits are a pest, a vermin, a quarry for hunters. And it was as hunters that my brother and sister and I had wandered over the brown hills on dusky Saturday evenings, following my father and the big old-fashioned twelve-bore double-barrelled shotgun. Later my brother had a gun too — a Winchester .22 — which he allowed me to use sometimes. The dead rabbits were very soft and heavy, and we used to slit one of the back legs and push the other through and thread the carcasses on a long stick to carry home. Our family was poor, and the meat was handy. We nearly always had baked or casseroled rabbit for Sunday dinner. 'Underground mutton,' my father used to say. My later years in England did nothing to change my attitude: at bedtime I would read my children the Beatrix Potter books, but I never could get worked up about myxomatosis.

The bright-eyed little character in the soup bowl, however, seemed to have no connection with those long-ago Saturday slaughters among the brown grasses and prickly lantana or with the diseased carcasses strewn across the Cornish kale meadows. He was pretty and Disneyesque, and he appeared, besides, to possess a degree of intelligence quite remarkable in a rabbit. That is to say he would come when called, sit up and beg, and suffer himself to be lugged about the streets by the children without protest. One way and another we lavished quite a lot of affection on him and on the whole, I think, he responded about as well as a rabbit can. We never did succeed in house-training him, but perhaps this was not so much perverseness on his part as an overestimation of his intelligence on ours. This, and a tiresome habit of chewing the legs of chairs, were the only complaints Sevasti ever had against him. She would mutter a little as she swept rattling showers of pellets down the stairs, but she would also bring bundles of fresh, juicy grasses every other day.

'Eeech! He's making good meat now!' she would say admiringly. Fat old Calliope from the corner shop would come puffing up the stairs twice a week, her apron filled with *radichi* and cabbage leaves. 'To make sweet flesh!' she would hiss knowledgeably. The labourer Mikailis scoured the rocky hillside above Agios Vassilias for milk thistles and brought them down wrapped in a white cloth the labourers use here to pad their shoulders under the drag-ropes of the heavy *karros* they pull.

The rabbit accepted all these offerings equably, and in a short time became huge and lethargic and preferred to spend his days sprawled languorously under the desk at George's feet. It was hard to remember how pretty and cute he had been such a little time before.

'If you don't eat him soon he won't taste so good,' said our friend Ioannis the carpenter. 'Old rabbits get a funny taste . . . rank . . . .'

(It was this sort of talk that had terrified the children for weeks past, to the point that whenever Sevasti or Ioannis appeared they would snatch up the Animus and dive for the street, where they would hide him down drain pipes, in the midst of coiled ropes on the decks of anchored caiques, among the flour sacks on a stationary *karro*, and even, once, among the peanuts in the basket of Dimitri the *fistikia* boy. The rabbit appeared to take no harm from these adventures, nor even to become nervous, as another rabbit might.)

I told Ioannis coldly that I would as soon consider eating one of my children. The enormity of this remark caused him to treat me warily for quite some time. I suspect that he spat three times whenever he entered the house.

After all the drama latent in the threat of knives, the end of the Animus was rather silly. He crawled through a gap in the balcony railing one morning (what possessed him to stir himself to such an energetic feat I can't imagine), fell on to the cobbled waterfront, and broke his neck. The grief of the children – racked by a passion of love and loss that was beyond their comprehension – was insupportable.

'There, there,' Sevasti crooned unhappily, desperate to find some means of consolation. 'I will make such a beautiful soup of your little rabbit. Georgios will go now to milk the ewe, and Fortini will bring fresh onions.' The violence of the terror and revulsion caused by this offer nearly frightened poor Sevasti out of her wits. I found her in the kitchen with a face as white as the children's, dashing cold water over the bedraggled black head of the Animus. 'Blessed Mother of God send us a miracle!' she prayed passionately.

News travels quickly on a Greek island. On the dangling heels of the Animus, as it were, came fat Calliope with a bunch of spring onions; Mikailis, whose regular supplies of milk thistles gave him the right to advise on culinary procedure; Ioannis, full of congratulations for this fortuitous solution to our moral scruples, and with a carafe of retzina to accompany the feast. The festive air of this party was quickly transformed to dismay. Greeks love children dearly, and they are among the races quick to recognize real tragedy when they see it.

'Po-po-po-po!' Mikailis muttered uncomfortably. 'I never meant that *you* should eat the rabbit, my darlings. I will take it away. You need never know *who* eats it.'

'I will take it, nephew,' muttered Calliope hoarsely. 'Irini does well enough at beans or macaroni, but a rabbit now . . . a rabbit needs a *cook* to get the best out of him. Besides, have I not fed this animal on the best, the tenderest *radichi*? If those thistles of yours have not soured his flesh, he will be . . . .'

'Fools!' Sevasti was crouched over the sodden bundle of fur like a tigress defending her young. 'No one will eat this animal. It is not the Australian custom. Can't you see that the children suffer? One of you must take it and put it in the sea.'

'The fish will eat it,' said Mikailis simply.

Ioannis, who had been vainly trying to establish contact with the two shocked and offended children, now put down the retzina carafe with an air of renunciation.

'There is only one thing to do,' he said solemnly. 'We must bury this animal.'

Old Calliope looked as if she might explode, but for the first time since the discussion began the children turned great swollen considering eyes on the assembled company.

'Do you mean . . . *properly*?' Martin's voice was a queer croak. He had reached the stage of hiccups.

'Oh, properly!' Ioannis promised recklessly.

Shane wiped the back of her fist across her nose, choked on a sob, and said, 'With a coffin and remembrances and *everything*?'

Ioannis gulped slightly. 'Everything,' he said staunchly. 'That is, if *Theia* Calliope has a box that is the proper size.'

Theia Calliope glowered at her nephew, blotched wattles working, but bereft of speech.

Sevasti said menacingly that she was quite sure *Kyria* Calliope had a box of exactly the right size. They would go together and fetch it immediately. As they went down the stairs she was whispering urgently in Calliope's ear.

'Since this is Greece,' said Martin pedantically, 'it will have to be an Orthodox funeral, won't it, Dad?' His face was blotched with tears, but his eyes were shining.

'Son, it will,' said George.

The rabbit was buried gloriously at dusk, in a cardboard box scattered with jonquils and daisies, and the minute tin and plastic crosses collected by the children from innumerable christening parties, and Shane's remembrances. George and I had by this time begun to feel rather silly, particularly as an earlier attempt by the children to bury their pet themselves had been thwarted by a band of nearly a hundred Kalymnian children, who had raided the burial party halfway up the mountain and routed it in their eagerness to participate in the *epiketheios sto kouneli*. However, the coffin and body had been brought back to the house, albeit a little battered, and to mollify the children in this second disaster we had rashly agreed to be present at the evening cortege. We were a little afraid of offending the religious sensibilities of the islanders, but hoped to overcome any danger of this by sneaking the box under George's jacket and strolling up the mountainside in a casual manner, as if we were taking an evening walk.

It was obvious from the large and grave assembly on the waterfront that such a subterfuge was no longer possible: the word had spread that the Australians were observing a curious national custom and the town had turned out respectfully to honour us.

Solemnly we turned down the alley where the wide concrete stairway ascends to the upper levels of the town. Solemnly the procession followed us. The children, either overcome by the dignity of the occasion or perhaps feeling that it was expected of them, began to weep again, snuffling away damply in the thick warm dusk.

Women leant in the yellow lamplit squares of doors and windows, or squatted in the cobbled streets beside their charcoal tins, stirring at supper pots. All the alley smelt of beans stewing in olive oil.

'What is happening?' they called as we passed. Hastily adjusting headscarves and aprons, they left their cooking pots to run after us. By the time we had reached the top of the stairs the procession was fifty strong, and all across the mountain slope dark figures were flitting among the scattered houses, converging on us. The children clustered close about Martin and Shane began to chant softly: behind us a woman took it up and tossed it, shrill and unexpected, down the massed moving line.

The ludicrous reason for the procession was lost and forgotten; we were caught in something else, an old rite whose meaning had melted in a time lost long ago but whose form was part of that dim race-memory we inherit at our births. That wild cry of lamentation was not for a stiffening rabbit: it was for Tammuz dead, or the springing red flowers where Adonis's blood was scattered, or a woodland king torn upon the sacrificial oak. Straining and stumbling on the loose boulders, we toiled up the dusk-wreathed mountain and the chanting rose deep and sad from a hundred throats. A boy with a torch – or a lantern or a candle or a blazing cypress brand – moved to the head of the line and led us on. High over the noble rock that soars above the town one star hung in the great blue night. I thought perhaps we were climbing to reach it.

We buried the rabbit under some stones halfway up the donkey trail that leads to Agios Petros. It was now quite dark and we had climbed nearly to the top of the mountain. Everyone seemed rather dazed and confused. The boy with the torch shone the beam on the rocks for us, and there was a note of hysteria in his high excited laugh as we hurriedly covered the Animus over. Shane set the box of 'remembrances' beside it, and everyone began to giggle and shout, and we all trooped down the mountainside in a mood of high hilarity. Only *Theia* Calliope stayed behind, carefully arranging a little cairn of rocks.

'That's so she'll know where to dig it up later,' George said. 'For stew.'

That was all there was to it. In the morning Ioannis brought another little black and white rabbit, and spent all day making a slatted hutch with a hinged door and a rainproof roof, and the next day Calliope came again with *radichi*, and Sevasti with fresh grass, and Mikailis with milk thistles.

Although we kept that rabbit for a long time we somehow never developed the affection for it that we had had for the first one. The children began to harbour more ambitious thoughts about puppies and donkeys. Ioannis, on the other hand, seemed to love the creature passionately, even when it grew into a gaunt loping sort of Gary Cooper of a rabbit, with ears that seemed grotesquely long even for one of its species. Sevasti, too, would pet it for hours, and never once complained of the litter of pellets that had to be swept up each day. For months Calliope and Mikailis continued to supply fresh food with a methodical solicitude their own children never knew. There was never any mention of knives or cooking pots.

At Easter the spring grasses were out to feed the Pascal lambs that every family had bought for the Easter Sunday feasts. By the end of April the hills were brown and parched and it had become a daily chore trying to find food to satisfy the rabbit's Gargantuan appetite. Mikailis reported worriedly that there were no milk thistles on the mountain. Sevasti would rise at dawn to scour the hillsides, but some days she would find nothing and on others only a few brown stalks. The *radichi* had disappeared from the market and lettuces were costly.

'We'll have to get rid of it,' George said finally, and, in some relief, I agreed. The children, utterly indifferent to its fate, said they would give it away to someone.

After wandering about with the huge animal – all of two kilos now, and in the pink of condition – they returned at lunchtime with the creature still in their arms. 'All the children's mothers said they couldn't afford to buy the proper food for it,' Martin explained in some perplexity. Nobody, it appeared, would have it.

'Well, for heaven's sake, they could – ' I stopped abruptly, realising what I had almost said.

'Oh, I told them what lovely soup it would make,' Shane said

96

callously. 'It was funny, Mummy. All the ladies crossed themselves and spat three times.'

Ioannis, white-faced but determined, for the first time openly criticised us. We ought to be ashamed of ourselves, he said. The rabbit, he added accusingly, knew no father or mother but us. It was, he went on with dignity, like Tarzan growing up among the orangoutangs, believing they were his own kind.

Sevasti turned her head away, performed her household duties with set shoulders and compressed lips, and further expressed her displeasure by never once speaking to us directly all day. The rabbit, guided perhaps by instinct to where loyalty lay, loped about at her heels, and every now and then she would pick it up and stroke its grotesque ears sadly.

Finally it was American Mike, an engineer on a sponging boat and probably the most materialistic of our Kalymnian friends, who was persuaded to take it. He was ready to go off to the African sponge-beds within a few days, and we thought the rabbit might make a nice farewell supper for him. By this time I had come to actively dislike the animal. If I could have found someone to kill it for me I would have stewed it with sadistic pleasure and picked the bones clean.

'Well,' I said brightly a couple of days later, 'how did the rabbit taste?'

American Mike pushed his cap to the back of his head and scratched his wiry hair. He looked rather sheepish. 'Well, to tell you the truth, Mister Charmian, we didn't get around to eating it after all. Fortini took on so, and that girl Maria of mine. Jesus Christ, Mister Charmian! *Women*! They said it would bring bad luck and I might as well go and drown myself now as kill that rabbit and then go off in a sponging boat to Africa. Funny,' he said thoughtfully, 'I never did hear that before; not about a goddam rabbit. It's something new they got into their heads.'

'Well, what's happened to the rabbit then?'

'Oh, it's still around the house,' he said. 'Fortini keeps feeding it leaves off the grapevine. She says there'll be enough to last until there's some grass or something about again.'

SPONGE BOAT

*

by George Johnston

Andreas watched the slow dribble of the red sand through the old-fashioned hour-glass, and wondered if they hated each other as much as they hated him.

There was a smell of hatred in the air, of mistrust and hostility; and there was a smell of death, too.

You could smell death. Once, in Karpathos, Andreas had known a man who could smell an earthquake coming.

He cocked his thigh over the thick tiller and let the boat take the circle slowly with the engine muted to a dull beat that had no echo from the flat, oily skin of the sea. Circling around it, the white rubber tube of the air-hose went into the water at the same stiff angle, as if it was a metal rod upon which the boat was pivoting. You could tell the exact centre of the circle by the place where, every now and then, a clot of air bubbles came up thick and round and glassy, like the eyes of frogs. The bubbles never seemed to quite break the dark crust of the sea.

Andreas watched the last grains of sand trickle through the neck of the glass, and he leant forward to meet the eyes of Costas the *colazaris*. Costas was in the bow near the diving ladder, squatting with his naked buttocks on the black-calloused heels of his bare feet, holding the signal line in two fingers and twitching it a little as if a fish were nibbling. The marline rope looked thin and delicate in the gnarl of brown fingers, as if the knuckles were

99

bad knots tied in the line. Along the thirty feet of deck, across the bare sunburnt bodies of the waiting divers, Andreas could see the black marks in Costas's mouth where the sun had split his lips open. It made it look as if he had been tattooed like an Indian, or as if somebody had made a drawing of the mouth and found it no good and crossed it out.

Andreas licked the dry, cracked pain of his own lips and wondered what *his* face looked like. There was no looking-glass aboard the *Twelve Apostles* and it was more than six months since he had seen it. That was a queer thing to consider. They all knew what each other looked like, but they'd forgotten the look of their own faces.

Costas stared for a moment at the bubbles coming up, then glanced back at his captain and shook his head slightly, shook it grudgingly, as if he resented the need for communication with a man he wanted to kill.

The sun struck a winking light in the empty upper bulb of the hour-glass; Andreas, looking down, saw that the sand lay quite still in the lower globe like a big clot of dried blood. Well, old Thomas was a safe enough diver even though he was a cripple and half crazy at times. Another minute or so wouldn't hurt him.

He looked over his shoulder as the boat circled slowly round the intermittent jet of bubbles. The sun was still fairly high above the hot, red escarpment of the Libyan coast, but they were on a deep shelf – thirty fathoms where old Thomas was working it, and dropping away even deeper into dark clefts choked with a thick tangle of weed – and by four o'clock the angle of the October sun would take what light there was away from the seabed. And that would be the end of diving for the day unless they went into the shallow inshore beds for a final run.

There was no particular expression in the captain's eyes as he looked over the rail to where the nets were trailing slow and turgid in the lee-water, all black and squashy with the sponges they had taken — poor sponges, not good enough to pay for the fuel they had used.

There hadn't been a movement of the signal line in the three minutes old Thomas had been down on the thirty-fathom shelf.

Cooped up for nearly seven months together, fourteen men in a boat not ten metres long in the summer heat of the North African coast — that could do funny things to people. Maybe by now they did hate each other just as much as they hated him. If they didn't then it would not need much to make them turn on him. It wouldn't need much — just a little something like this smell of death that hung around the boat; or something else you couldn't account for. That was the way things happened, just a little touch of something unexpected. And it was just as likely that they would turn on each other as turn on him.

'Sand!' came the impatient cry from the bow.

Andreas looked down at the still pool of red in the onion bulb of the hour-glass. 'Four!' he yelled back. 'Four minutes!' He gave the signal to haul in.

'It's his second dive,' Costas bawled resentfully. 'Three was plenty.' The *colazaris* muttered something under his breath as he gave three tugs to the line and began slowly to haul it in, hand over hand, dropping it in a neat wet coil behind him.

Andreas shrugged, but he could feel the sinew cords of his thigh tighten on the thick wood of the tiller.

The kid Petros, thin and brown like a knotted stick, lifted himself stretching from the deck and said something to the boat-boy, and the boy tossed a pail over the side and sluiced sea water over the brass shoulder-plates. The water made the metal spit and a little cloud of steam rose. Petros climbed into the yellow rubber suit and bent his head down for the boy to settle on the shoulder-plate.

Andreas tried to catch the eyes of Petros to see if there was murder in them also, but the kid kept his head turned away, saying something in a low voice to Costas.

Maybe they'd turn on him anyway, thought Andreas — maybe they'd do that whatever happened, because at least they knew where they stood when it came to hating him.

They hated him because for two years now he'd had the smell of death about him, and because bad luck ran with him just the way it had the season before. They hated him because in all the time they'd been at sea, cruising every bed from Alexandria all the way to Tripoli, there hadn't been a single day when the *Twelve Apostles* had made a take of worthwhile sponges. They hated him because they'd buried the drowned body of Big Petros in the sands near Derna before August was out, and had had to send two others back to Kalymnos, paralysed. And they hated him most of all because they knew he hated them, hated them and despised them for a bunch of bums and incompetents who wouldn't have got a summer's work at all if two of the boats hadn't been lost off Crete.

Nor, if it came to that, would he have got a boat to command, he reflected bitterly, because the bank had held up the advance of money until all the rest of the sponge fleet had sailed, and by that time all the best divers had gone and there wasn't a man left in the port but the cripples and the loafers and the ones no other captain would give deck-room to.

'Surface!' yelled Costas, and the thud and hiss of the air pump slackened its rhythm and old Thomas came dragging slowly in towards the boat, all swollen and yellow like a groper, and with the sun blazing like fire on the copper of the helmet.

It was a day in April when fat Skyros, the banker, came walking towards him as he waited in the coffee-house, walking high and springy on his two-tone shoes with the shine of the morning on him, to tell him that the bank had finally agreed to advance the money for the cruise. And he'd settled his thick, powdered neck down into the collar of his new nylon shirt and gone to a whole lot of pains to explain how tough it had been persuading his superiors to overlook the fact that Andreas had lost two divers on his cruise the year before and hadn't brought back much more than third-grade sponges. And Andreas had asked him rather tartly whether they remembered the five seasons before that when he hadn't lost a man and had filled the warehouses with more sponges than any captain sailing from the island. But the banker had just smiled to himself and taken a cigarette from his silver case without offering one, and that was when he had made it clear that if the two Thiakos boats hadn't been lost off Crete in the first week's diving there wouldn't have been an advance at all for Andreas's boat.

'You can't expect them to overlook another bad season, so you better be careful the way you pick your divers,' Skyros had said, smiling to himself as if he knew damn well that there weren't any good divers left in the port, although he did say: 'Right now the joint's full of bums.' Once upon a time Skyros had worked a few years in New York and he liked to use American expressions like that.

A sudden jet of angry voices from the bow jolted Andreas from his reflections.

They'd taken the helmet off old Thomas, and his bald, leathery head, all shrivelled up and brown, stuck out of the shiny brass circlet of the neckpiece like the head of a tortoise − a sort of angry tortoise, with its face screwed up and working − and what he was angry about was something to do with the kid Petros, who stood before him big and arrogant in the clumsy yellow suit waiting for the helmet to be put on. Costas was in it too; and Pavlos, one of the other divers, had jumped up from the deck, naked as the day he was born, and he was throwing his arms about and shouting at the kid.

Andreas touched the engine-lever back to the last notch of the throttle and set the tiller in its sling.

Maybe this was the little touch of something unexpected he had been thinking about.

Coming up, old Thomas had felt resentful, all the way up

from the shadowy blue-green and the streaky weeds, all the way up through the clear paling blue which always looked like the painted skies in the church icons, all the way up to the yellow twist and dapple of the sun below the surface water.

He could have stayed below another minute, maybe two – that was what made him feel resentful – and that would have given him plenty of time to crawl in over the rock ledge and through the weeds to where he could see the face of the white lady looking at him: not white really, but a sort of queer pale colour as if it had been white once before something had happened. Down there not enough light came through the water to see what had really happened to the white lady.

It was a sort of green light, although the dark twisting shadows that moved through it were more black than green, and the light moved in slow rippling ribbons that made it hard to see things clearly. But he had stayed there a whole minute crouched in the slime, staring across at the lady who looked at him through the weeds.

The weeds made it still harder, because they kept swaying backwards and forwards very slowly, twisting on their thick fleshy stems. Sometimes he couldn't see her at all for the weeds, and then her face and shoulder and breast would appear. Once all the weeds began to shiver and spread apart, as if they were live things and something had scared them, and that was when he saw all her body down to the waist, and a dark curving shape above her that looked like the hull of an old wreck.

And he had seen then just how the ledge dropped away into a deep chasm filled up with a thick blackness that was thicker and blacker than anything he had ever seen; but when he tried to see what it was the weeds swayed back and covered it over.

Somehow the resentment had passed when he got to the surface and he could feel them hauling him in with the sun-heat creeping through the metal of the headpiece and bringing the sweat into his eyes, and that was when he had grown crafty.

The lady in the weeds — that was *his* secret, and on his next dive he'd get across the ledge and reach her and find out what had happened to her. He had to make sure they dived in the same place, and that was why he had to tell the lie about the sponges. If they moved on to another part of the shelf he wouldn't see his white lady again.

'I tell you the sponges are there!' he screamed angrily, glaring into the cruel, mocking young face of Petros.

The kid spat over the side.

'Go down and see for yourself! There's a rock ledge slopes away . . . *big* sponges. It's covered with sponges, so thick you can't count 'em!'

'That's what I see.' The kid's pale, contemptuous eyes went to the netting bag knotted around the old man's waist, rested on the three shrivelled, scrawny sponges caught in the mesh, still oozing the black bottom-slime. 'You brought up plenty,' he said, and grinned.

'That ledge is tricky, I tell you.' Old Thomas was almost howling now with fury and panic. 'You got to get over weed patches, then under again. I didn't have time to — '

'You had time, all right,' Costas cut in sourly. 'Maybe you'd still be down there if I hadn't called.' The *colazaris* stared broodingly along the deck and saw Andreas had slung the tiller and was getting ready to come down. 'Fifty-eight metres I made it,' he added darkly, 'and that bastard gave you more than four without saying anything.'

'You don't get me diving fifty-eight for junk like that,' said Petros arrogantly. 'Not for shoeshine sponges. Better we run inshore now and do the shallow banks.'

'But I tell you the sponges are there!' Desperation gave a harsh roughness to old Thomas's cry. He had to go down again to find his lady among the weeds, and if they moved off now to do the inshore run . . . . 'They're like a forest down there,' he said quickly, half angry and half pleading, his voice choking into a sob as he said, 'More than we've seen all summer. When I dive again – '

'When you dive again it'll be on the inshore beds. We'll send someone down with you to stoop for you and pick things up.'

In the cruelty of the kid's words there was something fundamental, something vicious in itself that made Pavlos turn on him and take the side of the old man. He didn't care all that much for old Thomas, but he hated the youngness and the arrogance of the kid, and the way he'd become cocky on his first season just because he'd been lucky enough to pick up a few more sponges than anyone else.

'Maybe it'll be easier there for you too,' he sneered. 'Maybe it's safer where there's no slime and weed, only sand, eh? You dive one season and you know more about it than somebody who went to Tripoli ten years before you were born. You're pretty smart, eh?'

'Smart enough,' said Petros, and smiled coldly.

'Next season you try diving in a coffee-house back home. Worst that can happen is you might graze your elbow.'

'You want me to spit in your face?' said the kid coolly.

That was when Costas saw that Andreas had come up to them, and so he picked the right moment and said, 'Well, the kid's right, anyway. Now we go in and do the thirty-metre bank.'

'Who the hell is the goddam captain of this boat?' Andreas snapped. 'When we want your opinion on what banks we'll work we'll damn well ask for it!' He glared at Costas, but the *colazaris* met his eyes without expression. 'We stay right here while the light holds,' he said flatly, and turned to Petros.

'Put that damned headpiece on and get below,' he said harshly.

For a moment the queer thing that both of them wanted hung between them, unexpressed and vibrant, tasting of death and violence, and then it broke apart and Andreas was conscious of the insolent disdain in the boy's face as he said, 'Suppose you keep your eye on that sand-glass this time. I'd like to get up again before it gets dark.'

He turned away, bending over awkwardly in the patched yellow rubber suit and tilting his head to one side so the boat-boy could fit the headpiece in its lock-ring.

He'd always been a cocky walker, Petros, ever since he was a filthy little barefoot kid playing around on the Kalymnos waterfront, always in trouble with everyone, then getting rougher through his adolescence, with the police watching him all the time, waiting for him to step out of line.

It was sort of funny to realise, Andreas reflected, that he had been watching the kid growing up all the time, not paying much attention to him and yet watching him grow up out of the corner of his eye, you might say – and disliking him more and more as he grew older and cockier.

He could see the little scenes now, strung together like sponges drying on a line: most of them cruel scenes, like Petros on the breakwater behind the lighthouse grabbing the crabs the smaller kids had caught and crushing them to death on the rocks beneath his bare feet; or the time he had taken the tiny live sparrow-chick from the two little girls and thrown it into the sea, and had smiled as he watched it drowning while the two little girls ran away screaming and blubbering through the coloured houses. Once, walking in the later afternoon along the breakwater, Andreas had thought he might have been mistaken about the kid, because he had seen him sitting there all alone on the grey shingle by the slipways, and he had a little mongrel terrier in his arms and he was caressing it and crooning to it. But then the dog had run off to chase a stick and when the kid called to it, it didn't come back to him. And so he had pelted it with rocks and the pup had fled yelping away behind the Customs House.

Lately he'd grown nastier than ever – maybe that was

because he had a pretty good opinion of himself and he was sore because there was nobody to see how good he was except men who weren't any good themselves, anyway.

It was curious, he reflected, that back in Kalymnos before the cruise began the kid had been the last one he'd picked – and he wouldn't have picked him then except that there was nobody else about. And now he'd turned out the best diver of all of them, although that was only saying he was the best of a bad bunch. Although earlier, when the water had been warmer, he'd done pretty well as a skin-diver, going down naked with the big stone in his arms.

Maybe the kid was right after all; maybe he'd be really good if he was in a good boat and working with a worthwhile team. That was the sort of thing you could never be certain about. Sponge-diving was a funny business, and luck came into it.

Andreas watched the slow red dribble of sand through the neck of the glass while the boat slow-circled again, and his thoughts seemed to be measured out to the same slow rhythm: although maybe thoughts ran quicker than you realised because all this thinking about Petros had passed through his mind and not two-thirds of the sand had run.

And suddenly Costas was yelling from the bow and the line was jerking with the come-up signal, and they were hauling in with the sand still running.

'Why the devil did you come up?' Andreas snapped.

'I felt like a cigarette,' Petros said insolently, and turned away as if he was not interested in the conversation, and began to climb out of the yellow suit.

'Why you – '

'I came up because there was no point in staying down,' the kid went on, talking with his back turned to the captain. 'There's nothing there. Weed and an old wreck and soft ledges covered with muck. A few trashy scraps of sponges that stick to your hand like rubber. I didn't bother.'

'He's a liar!' old Thomas screamed shrilly. 'He's nothing but a damned liar! He's scared of the weed and the ledges, that's what it is! There's sponges there, I tell you, and *I* know where they are. I'll go down now and – '

'You damn well will, that's certain,' Costas cut in grimly. 'We're tired of hearing you scream about these wonderful sponges of yours. You get the gear on and go down and bring some up for us to see.'

'I will, yes, I will!' the old man gabbled eagerly. 'I'll go down now, yes, right away! I'm not scared of a few weeds on a soft ledge like some – '

'Ah, shut your mouth!' Petros said coldly, without turning his head.

'The truth hurts, doesn't it?' said Pavlos slyly. 'Even when you're smart as you are, baby boy, it hurts all right.' He moved in close behind the kid's back, square and chunky and threatening, his broad back muscle-tense and brown as old leather and pitted with the marks the salt-water boils had left. He was still naked but he had strapped around his thick waist the belt that held his fish knife. 'You get that suit off and take it easy, son,' he taunted. 'Soon we go inshore and find you some nice, hard, safe sand to walk around on.'

Petros turned his head slowly, his eyes empty of expression, and spat clean into the other man's face.

Pavlos's first punch splashed the kid's blood all over the yellow rubber of the diving suit and the second knocked him clear across the anchor bitts; but after that the kid kicked his legs free of the awkward garment and began to throw punches himself, and although the other man was bigger and stronger he had a quick way of hitting and moving away, and there was a lot of drive and sting in the wiry thinness of his arms, and it wasn't long before both faces were mashed up and ugly, and Pavlos was trying to get his hand down to reach his fish knife.

Andreas was not aware that a faint smile was playing around

his mouth as he watched them hammering at each other. They were standing almost toe to toe now, belting at each other, and there was blood all over their naked bodies and spattered across the deck planks and the gear, and nobody made a sound watching them, and there was nothing to hear but the fists thudding and the two men gasping and grunting.

The smell of death and hatred was spreading away from Andreas now: spinning away into a concentrated vortex of violence surrounding the two thrashing, naked, bloody figures on the foredeck. If he let them go a little longer the boy would grow tired and Pavlos would be able to get his hand down to the knife in his belt. Already the kid was slowing down; there was not much sting now in his short, jabbing blows, and he no longer tried to move away, just stood there quite stiff and straight, taking the punches wherever they fell and retaliating almost automatically. If he let them go for a minute or two longer . . . .

Andreas went in between them with his shoulder thrust forward just as Pavlos began to crouch with his hand fumbling for the knife, and he flung his arms wide with the fists bunched and sent both of them staggering.

'Break it up!' he roared. 'What the hell do you think this is? Get back to work, all of you!' He glared from one man to the other and the two broken faces looked at him dumbly, and the men packed around the bitts and the windlass and the forestay began to stir and fidget.

Andreas could feel authority in his hands again, a hard, shining thing like a jewel, and while he had it he clenched it tightly and shouldered aside the swaying figure of Pavlos with rough indifference, turning his back on the knife and the brutish violence that went with it.

'All right,' he said coldly, glowering into the vacant, bewildered face of old Thomas. 'What the devil are *you* waiting for? The *colazaris* tells you to go below you damn well go below. You know where these sponges are you get down there and bring 'em up.' Fear and supplication, or a sort of supplication, flickered for an instant in the old man's eyes.

'Get the gear on!' Andreas snarled mercilessly, and swung on his heel and glared towards the silent deckhouse. 'Air!' he yelled. 'Who told you to stop that pump?'

There was a quick scuttling noise from inside the deckhouse, and as Andreas strode back to the tiller the hiss and thud of the air pump seemed to mark his footsteps, and the eyes of every man aboard the *Twelve Apostles* watched him as he went.

There had been a queer, sick feeling in his stomach just for that one moment when he had turned his back on Pavlos and the knife. Only for an instant and then it had passed, but he had known that he was spinning with them in the very centre of that vortex of brutality and spite.

And there had been a red thread quite clearly running through it all, and running back to the little coloured house on the hill with the two women in black watching him secretly from the bedshelf and not saying a word. The thread thinned out there, but it still went running on, all the way back to that August day off Tripoli the season before, with all of them crowding the bleached deck planks to stare down at the drowned, blotched body of young Elias sprawled out in the heat, and the grotesque shape of the yellow rubber suit thrown over the winch like a cardboard cut-out that had gone soft in the water, and Vassilis the engineer down on his knees beside the engine-house weeping and cursing over the broken coupling of the air-line.

All this was tied to the glittering point of Pavlos's knife by the clear, red thread.

When Skyros had told him of the bank's agreement to advance the money it hadn't been all that easy to have to go looking for Pavlos to see if he would come diving, even though he knew that Pavlos would have to say yes because he was a poor man and his family was hungry. Even so, Andreas had hoped to find him in one of the tavernas where maybe they could have talked the thing out without too much resentment or bitterness, so that it was worse than ever when he had to go looking for him in the coloured cube of a house on the rock cliff above the church of Saint Stephanos.

The two women had been there, the wife of Pavlos and the widow of Elias, and both of them were still wearing black and watching him from the bedshelf not saying a word, nothing except 'Kalispera' when he arrived and 'Kalinikta' when he left. And Pavlos hadn't much to say for himself either. He had sat there for a long while under the lamp, picking at the bones of a barbuni, and maybe he was thinking there wasn't much food in the house apart from the picked-over platter of fish, because his eyes were sombre on the plate, or maybe he was angry knowing he had to say yes in front of the two women, knowing right from the beginning that he'd have to go sailing with the captain who'd drowned his younger brother Elias off Tripoli.

But Andreas had still had to ask him, and to wait for the answer, while the two silent women in black stared at him from the dark shadows where you could just make out the old lithographs of Genovefa, and the black left-alone eyes of Elias's little son watching him over the edge of the hammock.

That was the point where the red thread thickened, and that was pretty sure to be the reason why he had wanted to let the thing run its course when he had seen Petros and Pavlos hammering at each other, so that the kid would weaken and Pavlos would be able to come in with the long thin knife and cut the red thread.

But instead of that he'd broken up the fight, so that when he turned his back on Pavlos the red thread was still there, thicker and clearer than ever. The cause of the queer feeling in his stomach was really nothing more than waiting for the knife to come and cut the thread in a different way.

Andreas turned his head and began to whistle softly through

his teeth as he watched the glassy jets of bubbles coming up from old Thomas through the dark sea.

Old Thomas felt very pleased with himself because he had found the crusted spur of rock so quickly. It hadn't taken him more than a quarter minute to climb across it, and now he could see the lady, quite clearly too, because the spur seemed to run across to a clear lane cut through the weeds.

The weeds themselves were quite dark and thick, more like bunched fingers than plants, and you couldn't tell whether they grew out of sand or rock because they poked up from a sort of black fog that kept stirring itself around in the currents. Above the sediment and the weeds several shoals of smallish fish hung, quite motionless and almost transparent, but much more distinct than the bottom half of the picture, which looked as if it had been smudged. The queer thing was that the white lady was the clearest part of the whole picture, because even though she was maybe thirty feet away at the end of the lane through the weeds, you could see the way her skirt blew back from her thighs as if the water was rippling it, and the way she was toppled over a bit and bedded down into the thick slime. There was a lot of broken timber behind her that was crusted over like stone, and you could see the shape of the wrecked ship fading up into the blue movement of the water haze where the transparent little fish floated.

Thomas brought the air-line in carefully between his legs, stroking it down from over his shoulder, and began to move very carefully along the rock spur, bent right over and jabbing his fingers down in front of him, listening to the air whistling in the valve.

It had a queer shape, the wreck, round as a wine barrel and arching high up at one end where it hadn't broken away – something like one of the old boats you still came across occasionally sailing out of Smyrna.

The rock spur was still there beneath him, running clear to

the beginning of the lane through the weeds, and quite firm and solid even though the slime was thick and slippery on the top of it. It was the slime that made it tricky, because once or twice his arms were buried to the elbows before his fingers found the rock beneath.

There was a sort of strange, faint smile on the face of the white lady, as if she had just remembered something that had happened a long time ago and was waiting for Thomas to come up to her so she could tell him about it.

Thomas guessed that she was made of marble, because marble didn't seem to get crusted over the way other things did, and she reminded him of the time, years before, when the *Saint Demetrios* had lost her mast in the storm off Rhodes, and while they were in port making repairs they had gone along to the museum in the town and they had seen a stone statue quite like the lady in the weeds, with the same sort of smile, and somebody had told him that there was no way of knowing how much money it was worth, maybe thousands and thousands of gold pounds.

At first, when he began to feel the rock spur dissolving beneath him, it was such a strange sensation that he didn't feel at all frightened, only curious at how such a thing could happen. The rock didn't come to an end, or crumble, or break away, it just turned into a sort of paste and then ran away into a soft liquid like the sea thickened up.

It may have only lasted a second or so, the feeling of wonder, but the fear didn't really come to him until he saw the black, smudgy fog billowing up before his eyes, blotting out the peculiar smile on the face of the white lady.

It was only then that he could feel the cold claws of terror clutching at his throat and heart. There wasn't even the sensation of falling or sinking, just a slow going down like a light failing – going down and down, very slowly and softly, into the thick blackness, as if he were drowning in the ink of some gigantic squid.

The blackness before his eyes turned into a slow flood of red as his fingers began to jerk spasmodically at the signal line.

Petros took the big, smooth thirty-pound stone and lifted it once or twice, and he didn't seem to be listening as Andreas said:

'You got to work fast once you're down, son – and make up your mind fast too. Maybe with all that mud you won't see anything – you'll have to feel for him.'

'It's a damned sight more than mud holding him,' Costas said softly. He still held the marline line in his gnarled brown fingers and every now and then he tried to twitch it, but there was no give in the rope. The white tube of the air-hose and the thin brown line ran side by side into the sea, taut and still, like rods of metal.

The air pump was still thudding and hissing, but the bubbles were coming up in a queer fashion now, in sudden violent explosions broken by what seemed long periods when no bubbles came up at all, and then one or two big black clots would burst the surface as if parts of the sea had turned to liquorice.

The red sand was still running in the glass.

'If you can work him free we can drag,' Andreas said in a low voice watching the bubbles. 'But you got to make up your mind quick.' The bubbles coming up were all black now. 'If you can't work him free,' he said, 'you got to cut that hose.'

'No point in wasting all that rubber,' Pavlos said. He spoke as if he were talking to himself, and then nodded slightly as if he had found some special interest in the remark. 'Not on top of everything else.' He took the knife belt from around his waist and strapped it on to Petros as the kid began to climb on to the wooden rail beside the diving ladder.

'If you can work him free we can drag,' Andreas repeated, and looked up at the naked body balanced on the wooden rail, stake-thin and black against the burnt-out pallor of the African sky.

Petros nodded, but his eyes meeting the captain's were as cold and arrogant as ever. He lifted the big stone again from its nest of coiled rope and gave it three slow-swinging heaves to get the turns of the rope around his left wrist. His tongue came out to moisten his cracked lips, and it was a queer pale pink in the bruised and bloody face. He looked up into the colourless sky as he began to take his breath in.

He filled his lungs silently, swinging the big stone from the rope around his wrist, and then there was a sudden bigger swing and the stone was above his head, clutched in both hands, and he was over the side, headfirst into the water.

The *Twelve Apostles* rode motionless on the still, secret sea, and they looked down at the dark, thin, wriggling rush that faded and shrank as if it were pouring away down the pale cable of the air-hose, and then the splash frothed away and the bubbles boiled up like a comet's tail until suddenly there were no more bubbles, only the dark, thick skin of the sea closing quietly over its wound.

There was nothing to be seen of Petros now – nothing of Petros and nothing of old Thomas – only the rope kicking, kicking, kicking off its coils and running out, the coils spinning off and the rope hissing down into the sea, and then a last weak kick as if the life had been crushed out of it and the slack of the line sagging in the quiet, concealing water, quite close to the stiff, slender column of the air-hose.

Pavlos began to twitch the rope with his fingers, but it was quite loose in the water, as if there was nothing at the other hidden end of it.

The black sediment began to boil up at Petros even before he reached the bottom of his plunge, but it wasn't an even spread of black, like night or blindness. It had gaps of a queer green light in it and moving shapes that had no colour at all, and in the shapes there were bunches of weed reaching towards him like blunt, groping fingers.

116

He sensed rather than saw that the air-hose ran into the part where the blackness was most opaque, but it took him several seconds of fumbling around in the ooze before he found it, and then he had to unhitch the big stone from around his wrist so that he could get the leverage of both hands on the rubber, and then he kicked himself over and tried to find something to get his feet against.

But there was nothing to get his feet against and that scared him more than the blackness. The dark patches in the sea were something you got accustomed to even when you didn't like them, but there was always something solid on the bottom of the sea, and now the only solid thing was the rigid column of the air-hose and nothing beneath his feet but a soft, black ooze that went down and down and down for ever.

He could feel the air holding sweet and full in his lungs, and that made him feel quite a bit more confident, so he took a firm, twisty grip on the rubber hose and kicked his feet up to bring his naked body parallel with the hose with his head pointed down. And then, very slowly, he began to drag himself hand over hand down into the blackness. He could feel the air beneath his palms pumping through the hose like a soft heartbeat . . . .

There was no light at all now, nothing that was green or queer or shapeless, only a blackness such as he had never known before. He could feel the thickness of it on his skin.

Working between Thira and Crete on the way down to Africa they'd sailed one day over the *ifaísteio* where the volcano had blown the great gap-toothed hole in the bottom of the sea — and that had been the blackest thing he or any of the others had ever seen. They'd sailed on without doing any diving around those parts. But then they'd been looking down at it through the sun-dappled shimmer of forty feet of water, so that it really wasn't much more frightening than looking at a lion through the bars of a cage.

But this was different. This was different because you were going down into it, right down into the dark, bottomless belly of it all, hauling yourself hand over hand into the terror and the nothing of it.

Maybe this was an *ifaísteio* too – and old one from long ago all slimed and weeded over around the lip of the hole so you wouldn't know about it.

There was a throb of red now threaded across his eyes against the blackness, a running flow of little studs of pain and colour, as if an electric current was taking the pain in one ear and moving it across to the other.

Or maybe in this sort of blackness your eyes turned inward so you could see your own blood churning through the veins. The pain had begun to spread to his chest, just little needling pricks at first as if the casing of his lungs had turned into raw wool, and then a deeper, duller pain like bone being hurt.

His fingers had grown very cold, but he kept groping and fumbling down along the hose, trying to feel for the lock-nut of the coupling on old Thomas's helmet – but there was nothing to feel except the slimy column of the hose going down and down.

The blackness seemed to have grown a skin, because he could feel it all over his body like a smooth, thick coat, and it was flooding over him more and more thickly all the time, with a sort of jelly feel about it. He couldn't pull himself down any more.

He took his right hand off the hose, although it was quite an effort to pull free of its stickiness, and harder still to get his hand down and behind his back to feel for the knife in the belt around his waist, Pavlos's knife. When he felt it in his fingers he began to twist his body away.

It was a queer thing to be killing a man like this, in the darkness, with everything turned to black jelly.

Pavlos's knife was very sharp. It went into the hose as if the rubber was bread or a soft sausage, and when he twisted his wrist to make the slicing cut the air from the hose exploded the jelly and the blackness all over him as if the sea had burst apart.

He went up through a slow-boiling churn of thick bubbles that seemed to spin him round and round very gently, so that when he came out of the blackness into the green light and the weird shapes without colour he had the illusion that he was moving through the visions of a dream. They were strange pictures that circled slowly around him and dropped away: black balloons swirling and queer plants like groping hands reaching out to clutch him, and even the pale face of a woman who seemed to be smiling at him through the weeds, smiling at him as if she understood what he had done with Pavlos's sharp knife. And then the face wavered in a green ribbon of light and the weeds closed over it, and Petros knew that he had seen something that he could never tell to anybody as long as he lived.

With the last of his failing strength he began to kick his way up to the sunlight.

He surfaced with a great, sobbing gasp, his thin body jerking from the water all the way down to his belly, about twenty metres from the boat. But for quite a long time he trod water with his head turned away from them and tilted up a little as if he were looking into the pale, sun-bright sky. His eyes were tightly closed.

He turned on his side and began to swim slowly toward the *Twelve Apostles.*

There was no expression on the face of Pavlos as he began slowly to haul in the slack of the air-hose, bringing it in with a rhythmic, swirling motion so that the wet rubber tube fell in exact coils between his widespread legs.

The air-pump had stopped working, and no sound broke the silence but the soft, flaccid slap of the wet rubber falling, falling, falling. Near the forward bitts the boat-boy was wiping the grease off the spare diving helmet with a wad of cotton waste.

Andreas turned his head away and stared across toward the harsh coast of Africa. A light, offshore breeze had risen, stroking little flurrying fans of dark air across the water. The Libyan cliffs seemed as if they had been steeped in blood, and the shadows clotted in one big *wadi* running clear to the edge of the sea made it look like a gigantic scar in the earth.

The fitful gusts of wind had blown away all the smells – the smells of death and hatred and mistrust. There were no smells at all any longer; nothing but a queer feeling of peace and quietness that seemed to be folded around everything, the boat and the men and the sea and the sky.

The sand lay in the lower onion-bulb of the glass, dry and red and still. No bubbles came up from the dark water. *Sluk* . . . *sluk* . . . *sluk*: the rings of the rubber hose fell one upon the other, precise and rhythmic.

Andreas turned his head slowly and looked into the eyes of the kid Petros. Except that when you looked into his eyes you knew that he wasn't a kid any longer, because the thing you saw there was something that would stay there for ever now: for as long as he lived it would be there in his eyes.

Petros ran his tongue across his cracked lips and looked away. 'It's all right,' he said awkwardly. 'You don't want to worry.' He stared over the rail at the still water. 'There will be other seasons,' he said.

'Sure, there'll be other seasons.' Andreas nodded. There would be other seasons for Petros, yes, plenty of them. But there would be no more seasons for him. 'There'll be other seasons,' he repeated, quite softly, as if he were talking to himself.

Pavlos was bringing in the last length of the hose, holding it for a moment in his hand and staring curiously at the jagged cut at the end of it.

Andreas reached deliberately towards the engine wheel.

'We'll try two more runs inshore,' he said, 'on the shallow beds. There's still time.'

Petros looked at him.

'Well, what the hell do you want us to do?' said Andreas sharply, almost angrily. 'Just sit around and wait for those other seasons?'

Petros turned his head away so he wouldn't have to look at what was in the old man's eyes.

The *Twelve Apostles* turned on a slow circle and headed toward the coast of Libya. Astern of her a dark, muddy stain on the quiet surface of the sea heaved once or twice in the wake and spread away and dissolved.

ASTYPALAIAN
KNIFE

*

by George Johnston

Before telling of the remarkable series of incidents that befell Michael Tosaris after he bought the Astypalaian knife from a market stall in the Portobello Road, it might be well to explain who he was, why he was in London, and how he was susceptible to a purchase so improbable.

He was, as his name implies, of Greek extraction, although he had been born in the city of New York and had never seen so much as a Grecian urn until his studies at a school in Connecticut had imbued him with a vague interest in his classic heritage. He was, however, a young man more interested in figures than in fancies, and this first nebulous, half-guilty awakening was soon supplanted by a deeper interest in the curious economics of the country which had suckled his ancestors. The exports and imports of Greece and her seismic convulsions of inflation and devaluation excited him profoundly.

It was this interest that took him to the London School of Economics and, unwittingly, to the Astypalaian knife.

His father, who was president of the firm of Tosaris Maritime Inc., Ship Brokers and Marine Agents, was pleased that his son had so compelling an ambition toward the mastery of what the old man always referred to as 'facts and figures'. He naturally assumed that the boy's interest, aided by his more mature studies in London, would lead inevitably to a formidable business acumen and any number of lucrative directorships.

'He'll be sharp, that boy!' was the way he would put it over elaborate luncheons at the St Regis or less formal junkets at Toots Shor's.

He was a man of limited learning, and he did not know that all practising economists are as abstract, as impractical, and as visionary as any poet brooding over his images or any artist waiting to be moved by his sensory impressions.

Had he been aware of this, Anthony Tosaris would have gravely disapproved of his son's journey to London in search of academic distinction and material for a thesis already tentatively entitled *Greek Economics – A Cyclical Study*; because in the pattern of the born economist, the young man had decided on his theory before gathering his facts.

Old Anthony Tosaris had himself been born in New York. He had taken one vacation to the island of Andros, the birthplace of his father, but the visit had disheartened him considerably, for he had become involved with an old man who had insisted that 'nothing worth worrying about ever happens beyond the distance of a mule ride'. The incident had scared him and he had never repeated the visit.

It was Michael's grandfather, Mikailis, who had brought the sturdy Tosaris stock from Andros to New York, his hand clutching ten silver dollars, which was all the money he possessed in the world.

His young wife, a shy girl from Astypalaia to whom he had been married the summer before, survived two years in New York and died at the age of eighteen, leaving her husband with six-weeks-old Anthony and the task of compounding a fortune from their carefully hoarded savings, which had now grown to a total of one hundred and twenty-two dollars, one hundred of which Mikailis spent on a splendid funeral.

Sixty-four years later, on a cold November day in London, Michael Tosaris saw the Astypalaian knife on a stall of gimcracks in the Portobello Road.

Nothing of his family's link with Astypalaia was in the mind of Michael Tosaris when he made his purchase for the sum of two shillings and ninepence – a reasonable enough price to pay for what was to follow.

He was drawn simply by the bright look of the article, for the haft of carved charcoal-grey goat horn was inset with a simple design of little studs, some of brass and copper, others of tiny circles of bone dyed red and green and purple and yellow.

Michael paid his two and ninepence and stuffed the knife into his pocket with a queer feeling of guilty pleasure.

That evening, drinking mild-and-bitters with a fellow student, Simon Gideon, he inadvertently brought forth the knife while he was fumbling for his handkerchief.

'Ah!' Simon looked at it with interest. 'Yes,' he said, 'Astypalaian.'

Now Simon Gideon was an excessively tall and startlingly fair young Englishman of languid manner and immense self-possession. His subject, he boasted, was Greece. It was this that had first drawn him to Michael: later he had come to be distressed at his friend's singular lack of interest in the true values of his ancestors' land. Although Simon Gideon seldom appeared to venture far from his chaste little flat in Devonshire Mews he gave the impression that his whole life was spent in wandering from one end of Greece to the other. In fact, he had spent one summer there and had read extensively about Greece: it was difficult to reconcile his enormous erudition with the obvious fact that under the inclement Grecian sun his almost albino complexion would make him suffer raw blisterings of the most agonising kind.

'Astypalaian?' said Michael. 'How do you know?'

Simon smiled faintly. 'My dear chap,' he said deprecatingly, and left it at that.

'My grandmother came from there,' Michael said, remembering suddenly. 'From Astypalaia.'

'Ah!' Simon glanced at him warily. 'You know it then?'

'No. That's all I know. She was born there. I'd forgotten that when I bought it.' He shrugged. 'Well, I guess I didn't even know it *was* from there.' He carefully laid the bright little knife on the counter.

'A queer little island,' said Simon happily. 'These knives, that's about all they do. Primitive, don't you feel? But quite, *quite* pretty.'

'I don't know a whole lot about Astypalaia,' Michael admitted. 'I'm not even sure exactly where it is.'

'Oh, it's rather a poor lost little island.' Simon often talked like this, in a rather childlike fashion. 'Suspended in the Aegean, as it were, midway between the Cyclades and the Dodecanese.' He shook his head. 'Frightfully lonely. The people there won't eat fish with big eyes. Did you know that?'

'I didn't, no.'

'Oh, yes. There are only eighteen hundred people in Astypalaia. They're all uncles or cousins or something. Frightfully complex. And three hundred and sixty-six churches for a mere eighteen hundred people.'

'I've no idea,' said Michael.

'Nor have I,' said Simon cheerfully. 'The girls,' he added darkly, 'are practically kept in purdah. There are six or seven of them to every man, and – '

'Don't *all* fish have big eyes?' Michael said suddenly.

'I've never studied them particularly, old chap. Doubtless the Astypalaians are experts. They'd *have* to be if they had some rule of discrimination. Now, these girls . . . .' He paused thoughtfully, and after a moment turned to Michael. 'Listen, next summer I'm off to Greece with the Chivers. Why not come along? And then afterwards we could nip down to Astypalaia together.'

'Are you crazy?'

'You owe it to your grandmother,' Simon said nobly. 'You owe it to your grandmother and you owe it to your thesis.' He smiled quietly. 'You look after that agrarian economy, old chap, and I shall make a sociological study. I am drawn, I confess, by those girls. There is,' he added, 'a weekly *caique* from Patmos.'

There was. They went ashore from it on a sunny day at the end of May. There were three brightly painted boats in the harbour, two priests slowly climbing the long ridge leading to the monastery that dominated the town, an old man and a donkey sleeping together in the shade of a plane-tree, and a shepherd watching his sheep beneath the seven windmills on the crest of the hill. The only other sign of life in the little port of Pera-yaló, which is the capital and indeed the only town on the island, was a girl in a yellow skirt filling an earthenware pitcher at a communal well. She was strikingly pretty.

'Keep an eye on the bags, old chap,' Simon said, unnecessarily. 'I shall nip over and ask *her*.'

'Ask her what?' inquired Michael.

'I haven't decided.'

The street was paved with white sea pebbles, dazzling in the noonday sun, and Michael blinked as he watched his companion. Simon walked towards the girl, with the faintly melancholic smile that had always been so successful at Chelsea studio parties. Was there – he made the inquiry in Greek which, if a little stiff, was quite fluent – a reasonable hotel in the town?

'My friend and I are making a study of the island,' he explained, removing the melancholy smile and substituting a friendly twinkle. 'We shall want to stay here several weeks at least.'

There was no hotel, the girl told him in a soft shy voice that was pleasantly, even deliciously, musical.

'Ah!' Simon raised an eyebrow. 'One camps?'

It was the custom, he was informed in the same melodious cadences, for visitors to be accommodated either at the monastery or in some private house – if there was no objection to living with a family.

'Objection?' murmured Simon, injecting into his smile the

126

most devastating elements of his charm. 'I should like more than anything in the world to stay at *your* house.'

At this the girl seized her pitcher and fled.

In the meantime Michael had roused the old man with the donkey and – after a vain and stumbling attempt to elicit some information on the butterfat content of the local milk and honey output of the island – had also come to the point of inquiring about accommodation.

'*A-lah*,' said the man, whose very white hair and very blue eyes gave him the look of an old Spode plate, 'but what is to stop you from staying at my house? It's a fine big *spiti* and there's only me and the *yineka* and the six girls.' He called over his shoulder, '*Ella*, Heleni!' and then turned , shrugged resignedly, and rose to his feet. 'One of my girls was there, fetching water,' he explained. 'Now she's gone. Come. I'll put these bags of yours on the donkey and we'll go along.'

Off the track of the regular Aegean steamer routes, its rich red soil untrodden by the sneakers and wedge-heels of the tourist parties, the island of Astypalaia has both a considerable beauty and a quiet bucolic charm: it could scarcely have altered over the last few thousand years. In the first few days Michael found himself completely captivated by it.

In a queer way it all seemed to confirm the mental picture he possessed of his grandmother, who had died forty years before he was born. It was surprising that he *did* possess it: an image constructed entirely from a single yellowed photograph of a thin, shy girl with the face of a child.

This curious recapturing of a link which all his life had been lost to him was not the only reason he was glad that Simon elected to stay in the town during those first few days. He had a pressing desire to explore the little island alone. He was glad to escape from the cool white house by the harbour because of his embarrassment when he tried to pronounce the name of his host, which was Zarafonitopolous. Moreover, he had the task of talking to the shepherds and the farmers and the beekeepers, of questioning them on their output figures, turnover, methods of marketing, systems of conservation: of studying, in short, the agrarian economy of the island. It was necessary to sit with the fishermen overlooking the magnificent wide-reaching bay of Maltezana and find out all he could about hauls, man-hours, netting, taxation, packing, and prevailing prices, both whole-sale and retail, on the Piraeus markets.

It is a testimony to the insidious charm of the island that, while on the first day he filled twelve pages of his notebook with jottings and figures and the first draft of a statistical summary, on the fifth day his entries totalled less than half a page.

Indeed, he found himself sitting dreamily under an olive-tree on a cliff beyond the monastery, gazing at the sea, thinking how exquisite were the patterns of the wind ripples across the quiet water, how lovely the changing tones of green and blue and lilac, how luminous the dim and distant outline of Amorgos. He was aware of the drone of bees, the tinkling of the goat bells on the cliffs, the creaking of a windmill, the clatter of a cheese-press – and for the first time he was careless of their output or market potential.

His detachment from the bustle of Pera-yaló – if twenty-two donkeys, six fishing boats, and two bicycles constitute a bustle – consequently made him susceptible to surprise when, on his return to the house on the evening of the sixth day, Simon took him aside with a secretive air of foreboding and whispered:

'There is, I'm afraid, awful news, old man. A worm in the apple!'

'A *what*?'

'Do you realise we're being trapped?' Simon glanced over his shoulder, but there was only a brown goat champing its beard from side to side and eyeing him impassively. '*Trapped*!' he repeated darkly.

'Trapped?' echoed Michael, perplexed.

'But quite definitely! We should have seen it from the outset. I could kick myself! Can't you see they all think we're frightfully rich? Well, you *are* frightfully rich, but that's not the point. They think we're both frightfully rich, and of course they want to marry off their daughters. To *us*, do you understand?'

'But we don't have to, do we? I mean – '

'Old whatever his name is – Mr Zed – don't you realise that was why he was so anxious for us to stay with him? Six daughters, and not a man in sight – until *we* came along! *Six* of them, Michael! And only one of them personable. The rest of them – good Lord!'

'Which is the personable one?'

'I beg your pardon?'

'I said, which is the personable one?'

Simon stared in wordless astonishment.

'Well, I think they're all very kind and sweet,' Michael went on carefully. 'I wouldn't care to – '

'You mean you've never even *looked* at Heleni?' Simon measured out the words accusingly.

Michael considered the matter for a moment. Because of his trouble pronouncing the names he was not quite sure which one *was* Heleni. 'Which is she?' he asked.

'Oh, my Lord!' Simon groaned. 'But she's absolutely smashing! Are you blind?'

'I think all of them are nice,' Michael insisted stubbornly.

'We're not concerned with *all* of them – not at the moment, anyway. Because it's on the matter of Heleni that we rather touch the whole point.' Simon again stared over his shoulder into the yellow innocent eyes of the goat. 'I'm afraid there's been a bit of a misunderstanding.' He coughed. 'You see, *I* think that *she* thinks that I want to marry her ... well, to become engaged to her anyway, and ....' He smiled wearily.

Michael looked at him. In his baggy shorts he seemed to have grown to a height of seven feet. His eyebrows looked like twists of string. The skin was hanging in little strips from his nose and forehead, revealing subcutaneous areas of a blotchy rose-pink. He looked more like a bedraggled tropical bird of the stork family than a young Lothario.

'Well,' said Michael, 'if you like the girl, why don't you? If it doesn't make sense you can always call it off, take a boat out.'

'Actually it's rather more tricky than you think. In the first place I don't really think I want to be married just yet. And if you just become engaged to a girl here you're not allowed to *look* at her again until the day of the wedding. She goes into purdah or something. You do see that that would be frightfully awkward here – I mean with us all living together – and besides I like looking at Heleni.' He frowned. 'Yet I suppose we must be practical. Michael, I've come to the conclusion that it's just about time we up-anchored and off.'

'But we've only been here six days! Besides, I'm beginning to like the place.' Michael grinned. 'I guess another two or three weeks here won't get you into jail – or get your throat cut by an irate father.'

'Hmmmmm.' Simon glanced at him speculatively, and took a deeper breath. 'As a matter of fact,' he said quietly, 'you haven't heard it all yet. I'm afraid there's . . . there's another girl. It's rather involved, you see. She's the daughter of old Dimitriadis, who keeps the coffee-house down the street. Very small. Be-witching little thing. Her name is Artemesia. Quaint name, terribly archaic. She fought at Salamis you remember. Not this one, of course, the ancient one.'

'And she thinks you're going to marry her too, does she?'

'Something like that, old chap,' said Simon morosely. 'There is beginning to be some sinister talk about *brika*. That's their word for their dowries. I tell you they don't give you a chance!' His eyes searched Michael's desperately, and then he looked away and said awkwardly, 'I suppose I'd better make a clean breast of the whole thing. You see, there are a couple of others as well.

direction or disappear hurriedly behind the wall of a house. For a girl said to be 'hurling herself' at a potential husband, she was remarkably elusive.

Indeed, by the afternoon of the fifth day Michael was almost prepared to abandon the attempt as hopeless, and to accept Simon's more cowardly solution of flight from the island.

To consider this idea, he had taken himself on a solitary walk round the russet cliffs that walled in the shining bay. There were no valid reasons why they should not leave, he told himself miserably. He seemed, unaccountably, to have lost all interest in the agrarian problems of the island: the notebook for figures and statistics remained in his pocket – neglected, forgotten, rather grubby and a little dog-eared. The cyclical theory upon which his thesis was to have been built now seemed rather ridiculous, even vaguely presumptuous.

Silently he trudged through the gorse and the sweet-smelling herbs, afflicted by a restless melancholy. The very beauty of the landscape had somehow acquired a forlorn quality, its empty loneliness dominated by this figure of a girl with blue eyes and nut-brown hair.

Michael stopped, astonished by the course of his own reflections. He had not realised how vividly her picture had come to be impressed upon his mind. It was simply explained, of course: it was this stealthy and unremitting surveillance to which he had subjected her for the better part of a week. Yet could it *quite* explain the overwhelming clarity of the image that filled his mind? And there was some queer quality in it, too, that recalled that earlier, surprising thing: the landscape had evoked, with a vividness no less clear, the image of the Astypalaian grandmother he had never known. Were they alike, perhaps? He tried to recall the old yellowed photograph, but it was the picture of Heleni that dominated his imagination.

The mental surprise occasioned by all this was followed, only a few minutes later, by a physical shock even more startling. For he had gone on and climbed to the crest of a stony ridge and there on the clifftop rocks above the sea, fifty yards from the trail, was Heleni herself, watching the seventeen Zarafonitopolous goats. Except for the idly cropping animals, and a stiff-winged seagull cruising above her head, she was quite alone.

Michael lit a cigarette with studied nonchalance and walked towards her. She could hardly evade him this time: the cliff behind her was a sheer drop of four hundred feet to the rocks below. It was not likely that she would take flight and leave the goats to look after themselves in a position so dangerous.

In fact, although she lowered her eyes after her first quick soft smile of greeting, she seemed perfectly composed. He had not expected this attitude, so instead of being brusque and down-to-earth, as he had planned, he found himself talking inanities like: 'It's very lovely here', and 'Do you come often to this place?' and 'The goats look swell, don't they?' Her answer to each was a nod and a slow smile.

Michael flicked the cigarette away, coughed, and said, 'I've been wanting to talk to you . . . er . . . .' He had almost called her Heleni, which would have been a false step, but the more formal alternative was utterly unpronounceable, and merely to call her *thespina* had a sort of stiff school-teacherly ring to it. 'To talk to you,' he repeated lamely.

'You have been looking at me and following me all this week,' she said softly. 'But you do not say anything to me.'

'Oh, I had to talk to you *alone*,' he said quickly. 'It's . . . it's a sort of private thing . . . sort of awkward. It's . . . .' He took out another cigarette and tapped it rapidly against his thumbnail. 'It's about your wanting to marry my friend Gideon,' he said forcefully. 'That's what it's about.'

'*Kyrios* Simon?' She stared at him wonderingly, a little smile of perplexity touching her eyes and mouth. There was no doubt, Michael reflected, about her loveliness.

'Sure. He told me. I just wanted to say – '

'I think you have made a mistake,' she interrupted gently. 'I do not understand how you made this mistake, but, no, I do not want to marry *Kyrios* Simon.'

'Of course you do!' Her denial had given him a strange kick of relief, which in itself was puzzling, so that his accusation was made with a sort of emphatic defiance. 'Of course you do! If it comes to that I guess there isn't a girl in the town who doesn't. That's why I wanted to warn you that – '

He broke off abruptly. She was laughing.

'What's so funny – ?' he began.

'Yes, it would be funny,' she said, trying to keep a straight face, although her eyes were dancing. 'To marry *Kyrios* Simon, that would be very funny. Those *pantalonnia* he wears – '

'His shorts?' Michael smiled stiffly, conscious of the need for loyalty both to his friend and to the outer world of sophistication. 'In foreign parts, *all* Englishmen wear shorts,' he said gravely. Simon's, he was obliged to admit, were stranger than most, but the principle remained.

'There he is now,' Heleni said, pointing to the trail above them. And there, sure enough, was Simon, a gaunt, long-striding figure swinging his thin arms, moving at a considerable pace from one ridge to the other. Was there – Michael tried to remember – was there a bird in Africa or India called the apothecary stork? On one leg of Simon's shorts the hem had come away and the loose cloth was flapping around his knee.

He disappeared over the ridge without seeing them, his attitude that of a man distraught.

Scarcely had he vanished before a second figure appeared against the skyline: a fierce-looking man in a yellow coat who mopped his face with a red handkerchief as he hurried past, travelling in the same direction as Simon.

'And who is that?' Michael asked interestedly.

'Georgios. Georgios Dimitriadis. He has the coffee-house.'

'Ah, yes,' said Michael, remembering. 'And a daughter called Artemesia?'

'Yes.'

Before the full implication of this could be absorbed, the loneliness of the setting suffered a further intrusion, for a third man had appeared, following close on the heels of the coffee-house proprietor.

He was a stocky man with a flamboyant moustache, wearing the knee-boots and flat hat of the mountain farmer. Every few yards he would break into a trot. They could hear him panting. Michael turned a questioning face to Heleni.

'Lazarus Konis,' she said. 'He is a farmer. He brings the milk to us.'

'Oh, no he doesn't. It's his daughter Penelope, isn't it?'

'Usually, yes.' She looked at him in surprise. 'How is it that you know so many of these daughters?'

He had almost decided that it would be wise to tell her the full story when he caught sight of Simon, coming over the ridge again, returning towards the town at a long, loping trot, head down and thin arms working like pistons. The hems were down now on both legs of his shorts.

A few minutes later Dimitriadis and Konis also came over the ridge together, arguing heatedly. In true Greek fashion, they quarrelled with great fury without looking at each other, addressing their impassioned denunciations, pleas, threats, accusations, and exhortations to the rocks and shrubs and trees beside the trail.

'And what would you say all *that* was about?' Michael murmured as the wildly gesticulating figures disappeared from sight.

'*Fasoria*,' she said calmly, and shrugged.

'Look,' he said suddenly, 'I guess we'll have to discuss this other business later. I had better get back and see what this is all about.'

Simon was in the courtyard, crouched in front of a mirror

propped against a hibiscus in a pot. He was dabbing lanoline on his shredded nose. The reflection in the mirror was a picture of concentration until it caught sight of Michael, when an aggrieved expression came over it.

'Look, old chap,' it said querulously, 'I *do* wish you'd hurry up with that Heleni business. Time and tide, you know . . . .' He shook his head. 'You've been the better part of a week already, and absolutely nothing to report. It's hardly good enough.'

'Good Lord! It's *your* mess, not mine. And today's the first chance I've had to have a talk with her. It might interest you to know,' he added coldly, 'that she never intended to marry you.'

'Nonsense! She's playing foxy. Or setting her cap at you. Watch out, old chap! Anyway, if you *could* bash on and clean it up quickly and start working down the list I'd be uncommonly grateful. Others, you see, are becoming importunate.'

'Sure, I saw two of them. They looked mad as hell.'

'With each other, you mean?' He turned, frowning at a dab of ointment on his finger, and then he smiled. 'At the moment I've succeeded in turning them against each other. It won't last, of course. That's why I'd like you to step up the tempo a shade with Heleni.' He examined his clean shirt carefully before putting it on.

'You dressing up?' said Michael.

'Calliope.' He smoothed his fingers down the bridge of his thin, shiny rose-pink nose. 'I'm expected.'

Michael's anger simmered until they were eating supper and he heard Heleni tell her mother that she would take the goats next day to the same place on the cliffs because the grazing was good. She said it in quite a loud voice, as if she had intended him to hear.

It was, he realised, almost a perfect Aegean afternoon. A light breeze from the north fanned the sea out from the shore in an ever-deepening tone of blue, and the gulls were lazily swinging in the warm air. In the little harbour below there was a lethargic movement as natives trundled down the barrels of honey and crates of cheese to the Patmos *caique*. The *caique* had a yellow hull and pink masts, and the deckhouse was blue. The shade was cool and milky beneath the olive-tree, and the jangling of the goat bells all around them was a sleepy sound. He turned to Heleni, who sat clasping her knees and chewing on a yellow stalk of grass as she stared down at the harbour.

'If you don't want to marry him, is it because you want to marry me?' he asked softly. 'That's what *he* said. It's not my theory.'

'No, I don't want to marry you,' she said, her eyes on the Patmos *caique*.

'Why not?'

'Because you're rich. *Kyrios* Simon said you were rich. Very rich.'

'*Kyrios* Simon talks too much,' Michael said acidly. 'I'm not rich. My father is. That isn't the same thing. My grandfather was very poor, and he came here and married a girl from Astypalaia and took her away.'

'That's why I wouldn't want to marry you. Because you would take me away from here, and I don't want to go from here.'

'Sure,' he said, and closed his eyes.

It may have been a minute or an hour later when she said, 'The Patmos boat is going.' He sat up, blinked and saw the boat slipping around the end of the breakwater. Two men were hauling up the patched brown sail, and even from this distance he could hear the thin muffled thudding of the canvas.

Heleni reached beneath her yellow skirt and from a pocket in her petticoat produced a rumpled envelope and handed it to Michael.

'What's this?' He looked at her, but she turned her head away quickly.

'*Kyrios* Simon asked me to give it to you.' Her voice was low and nervous. 'He is on the Patmos boat. He made me promise not to give it to you until the boat had sailed.'

'He's *gone*, you mean!' He jumped to his feet and stared down. The *caique* was leaning slightly to the wind, and her wake was a thin silver wedge trailing back to the breakwater.

'He said you would not be angry!' Heleni stared at him in alarm. 'I did not want to . . . he said you would not be angry . . . he said . . . .'

But he was thumbing open the envelope. The note inside was brief:

> Loath to leave you in the lurch, old chap, but no other course. Reliable local tradition credits Calliope's father with enviable reputation as famous guerilla fighter and deadliest of marksmen. His tally: thirteen Turks, two Germans, five Italians. No English to date: desolating experience to be the first. Last night he sat watching me for two hours, *oiling his gun*! In the circumstances, know you will understand. London is sooty and smelly, but oh, it's so safe! In frantic haste.
>
> — SIMON
>
> P.S. Entirely your business, of course, but if you could possibly see your way clear to marrying one of them, it would rather do something to save face, don't you think?

Michael folded the letter and stared at the dwindling outline of the schooner, and then he thrust the envelope into his pocket and his fingers touched the little Astypalaian knife he had bought in the Portobello Road. He took it out and drew it from its sheath and began to whittle an olive twig.

'Are you angry now?' she asked softly.

'Angry?' He looked across the blue bay to sea-swallows whirling above the monastery. The Patmos *caique* had cleared the western cliff and vanished; the water was quite still and so clear that he could see the shoals and weed patches and the ribs of sand below the surface. A faint smile touched his mouth. 'Not angry,' he said. 'Just thoughtful.'

'There is no other boat for a week.'

'No.'

'Did *Kyrios* Simon say something in the letter to make you thoughtful?'

'He said a whole lot.' Michael grinned and turned to her. 'For instance, he insists that I marry you.'

'Marry me!' She sat up very straight. 'How can *he* insist on such a thing?'

'Ah, but he can, Heleni. You don't know *Kyrios* Simon.' He took her hand in his and tapped the back of it with his forefinger to emphasise his words. 'He looks quite young, but he isn't, you know. He's really my – well, my foster father. He acts for my father because my father lives in America and is very busy being rich. But if *Kyrios* Simon says I have to marry you, well then I must. Since he has been here he has looked at a great many girls of the island, but it is *you* he has decided on.' He shrugged. 'There's nothing I can do about it, Heleni.'

'But . . . but . . . .'

'It's no use, Heleni. He says I must marry you. He says I must stay here and live with you. This means, of course, that I won't be rich, but there's nothing we can do about that either.' He looked at her earnestly. Her eyes were the colour of the sea where the ribs of sand rippled below the surface. '*Kyrios* Simon is very strong willed. If we don't do what he tells us, he'll come back and he'll be very angry. If he makes up his mind to a thing, I guess we have to make the best of it.' He smiled at her. 'How old are you, Heleni?'

'Eighteen,' she said.

'When my grandmother was married she was only sixteen. But I think maybe she looked a bit like you.' He took a thicker twig and began to strip off the bark with the Astypalaian knife.

'That knife,' said Heleni. 'It is one of the very old pattern. They do not make them that way any more. You are lucky to have one of the old ones.'

'Very lucky,' said Michael.

'For when I am married,' Heleni said softly, 'I have twenty knives and twenty forks and some small spoons which my uncle made for me. They are very pretty, but they are not of the old pattern, like your knife.'

'Well, let's keep this one just for whittling,' said Michael, 'when we're thoughtful or happy.'

There is an old American adage – or is it from Lincoln-shire? – which runs something like this: *Clogs to clogs in three generations.*

To me it had always had a rather spiteful, malicious con-notation until my visit last summer to the island of Astypalaia. For the happiest man I have ever seen in clogs – although he was barefooted at the time, trampling between his vines in the wet red soil – is Michael Tosaris.

He has twenty-six acres planted with vines, figs, melons and *fragosica*, and two miles of cliff pasture for the goats. That evening, as we sat on the edge of the well, watching the sun go down in a boil of flame behind the monastery, he told me that he was applying modern methods of economics to the local agrarian economy and to cheese-marketing in particular. He was very excited about a new wine he was trying to develop, a *vin rosé*. He is, I imagine, the happiest Tosaris in three generations.

After sundown we feasted at the big bare table, with the bowl of grapes and figs in the centre and Heleni's tall candles casting a mellow light on the little coloured studs of the Astypalaian knives and forks; and the fish were gleaming and golden in the platters of oil.

The little knife of the old pattern was fastened to the white wall between the icons, like a talisman.

STRONG-MAN
FROM PIRAEUS

*

by George Johnston

Dimitri had never really been aware of the fickleness of women until the strong-man came from Piraeus. Because he was a Greek, he had always been inclined to take women for granted: an attitude which Hollywood films have dispelled effectively from such cosmopolitan centres as Athens and Piraeus, but still tenaciously held by the islanders, whose cinematic appetites are sustained by occasional showings of *Birth of a Nation*, *All Quiet on the Western Front*, and the earlier comedies of Laurel and Hardy, with Greek sub-titles.

And Dimitri was an islander. Not just another person who happened to be living on an Aegean island – a lot which may befall any spinster archaeologist from Milwaukee or scoutmaster-poet from Weston-super-Mare – but a very particular sort of islander. For Dimitri had been born and bred on a comparatively small and extremely barren rock called Kalymnos, which lies among the twelve islands of the Dodecanese group, ten miles from the coast of Anatolia and at least a million from all things sophisticated. No ripple of emancipation has yet reached this island, and its men accept the taking of women for granted almost as a matter of gospel.

Women, according to the strong and handsome Kalymnian men – and certainly to Dimitri, who was as strong and handsome as any of them – were soft and garrulous creatures who cooked food, sewed clothes, contrived patches, attended church, washed the clothes at the public wells and the rugs on the rocks by the sea, had babies, attended to them, obeyed all the whims of their husbands, and were always there when they were wanted.

They were not permitted to smoke or to drink with their men in the tavernas which catered for the masculine dominance of the island with vinous prodigality. In summer, if it was very hot, they could be allowed to bathe in the sea, provided they remained in areas rigidly segregated from the men, and even then only if their bodies were enveloped in concealing *fustani*, which had the appearance of old-fashioned nightshirts. If they could overcome in any way at all the trammelling stricture of these floating casings, their aquatic exercises were confined to the dog-paddle, breast-stroke, or mere dunking, the over-arm or Australian crawl being frowned upon as 'forward'.

On an island shunned by tourists as much for its aridity as for its token forms of sanitation, few influences calculated to alter this outlook had ever drifted as far as Kalymnos.

The men thought more about sponges than they thought about women, Kalymnos being the centre of the Mediterranean sponge-diving industry. Dimitri, in fact, had married Nomiki without giving any special attention to the matter: it was an arrangement their parents had made when they were still at school. The girl was industrious, an excellent sempstress and of a pleasant, good-humoured disposition. She had a nice singing voice and could perform the Kalymnian dances with liveliness and grace. And she had brought to the marriage a gratifying *brika* consisting of a small cottage on the hill above the harbour (lime-washed a pale blue and with yellow shutters and doors and a trellis of grapevines), all the necessary household needs and furniture (including a fine kitchen dresser), two Swiss oleographs which her grandmother had bought in a moment of rare and irresponsible opulence, a framed set of violently coloured lithographs depicting the adventures of Genovia, a white goat, and eleven brown hens.

Dimitri had not realised until seven months after their marriage that his wife was beautiful. This realisation he had never thought of conveying to her, although it had disturbed him a little at the time, as if he had suddenly discovered that the big kitchen dresser of which he was so proud was afflicted with the boring-worm.

The strong-man from Piraeus did not apply himself to the correction of this situation with any missionary zeal. His attitude to women, admittedly, was profoundly different from that of the Kalymnian men. He had drunk *raki* with a belly-dancer in Beirut, had two girl friends of his own in Turkolomani (who accommodated him in the friendliest possible fashion when they were not preoccupied by the companionship of visiting yachtsmen), and numbered among his acquaintances a juggler who had been divorced by his wife. The strong-man had a distinct regard for himself as a man of the world, but he was in no sense a missionary, a crusader, a reformer. He was, in fact, really zealous about nothing but the expansion of his chest, the size of his biceps, and his ability to loosen drachmas from the pockets of his audiences by such feats as bending steel bars across his forearm, straightening horseshoes with his bare hands, biting nails in two, and escaping from impossible situations when, seated in a chair, he was roped and chained by experts.

He was a swarthy handsome man, although rather short in stature, as if people had for many years been trying to hammer him into the ground as part of his repertoire, and he had a stiff, muscle-bound gait.

Dimitri saw him come ashore in the black caique that brought the passengers off the *Karaskaikas*, and immediately recognised the squat figure and that unmistakable muscle-bound walk as belonging to one of the cooks who had been attached to the Greek battalion with which he had served with some considerable distinction at Rimini.

It was this fact that prompted him to hail the man with a

joyful cry of recognition and welcome. In all the thirty-six years of his life, Dimitri's one day of pure glory had been that day when they had attacked the German posts at Rimini, surpassing even that later occasion when the King himself had pinned the medal to his tunic. His welcome to the strong-man was accordingly dictated by a sudden blazing desire to finger again the texture of this finest of his hours in the companionship of somebody who had been there too. It was not derived from any special feeling of affection at seeing an old army comrade again: Dimitri, indeed, had a vaguely uneasy recollection of having disliked this particular cook even beyond the normal call of dislike for army cooks in general. Nonetheless, Rimini was Rimini.

'Costas!' He hurried across the quay, his hand outstretched, greeting his old comrade exuberantly. 'Costas Kudaris!'

'Hercules,' the strong-man corrected equably. 'Fancy you not remembering! A long time, eh, Dimitri?' He smiled and lowered a meaningful glance at the long canvas bag at his feet, the bag containing the carefully softened horseshoes, the un-tempered steel bars that would bend with reasonable ease, the long nails doctored to an almost digestible condition of pliancy. And, sure enough, in large painted letters on the bag was the name, *Hercules Kudaris*.

'You must come to my house and eat with us,' said Dimitri impulsively, because he was not a particularly quick-witted man and it had unsettled him, making a mistake about the name. And by then it was too late anyway to withdraw the invitation because the man had accepted it very quickly.

As Dimitri led the way across the *plateia* he was rather silent and preoccupied. He had begun to remember some singularly distasteful incidents connected with the cook at Rimini. More-over, he had suddenly realised that this was Nomiki's day for *fasolia*, and there was nobody in all Greece with Nomiki's magic touch so far as *fasolia* was concerned. Would there be enough to go round three of them? His sidelong glance appraised the huge swinging shoulders of the strong-man. It was obvious that here was a creature of majestic appetites who could go through a whole potful of *fasolia* and then wonder when the *barbunia* was coming on.

Climbing up the hill, Dimitri consoled himself with the thought that it would at least be a good opportunity for Nomiki to hear about Rimini again. He was rather put out, however, to discover that the strong-man remembered nothing of the attack on the German redoubts – possibly he had been too busy watering the stew or black-marketing the battalion rations to Italians behind the lines – and when he reminded him of his own modest share in the battle and his decoration for gallantry, the strong-man raised his eyebrows and laughed in an amused, knowing way as if he suspected that Dimitri had invented the story just to impress him.

By the time they reached the blue house on the hill Dimitri had recaptured almost all the nuances of dislike he had felt for Corporal Kudaris in the old days of their Italian campaigning. Moreover, he was now quite certain that his name *was* Costas, because thinking of him as Corporal Kudaris he had suddenly remembered the men in his platoon always saying, 'That bastard Costas!' whenever the food was more foul than usual.

'This is Costas Kudaris,' he said determinedly, presenting Nomiki to him. With the infallible instinct of her sex, Nomiki was wearing her best white blouse.

'Hercules,' the strong-man corrected, and bowed, lowering his cropped bullet head over Nomiki's hand and kissing it. He had no neck, Dimitri realised, only the cropped head poised on huge shoulders that had to be twisted sideways to enter the narrow yellow doorway. Dimitri was a head and a half taller and had to take off his black peaked sailor's cap and bend his head to pass beneath the lintel, but it wasn't the same as having to twist your shoulders sideways to get inside. The *fasolia* smelt wonderful.

Throughout the meal the visitor talked a great deal about his travels and his prodigious feats of strength, addressing all his conversation to Nomiki, and there was not much opportunity to talk about Rimini, even had Dimitri wanted to, which he no longer did because of the acute depression that afflicted him watching the strong-man spooning up the *fasolia*. Whenever there was a pause in the monologue the man's gaze, Dimitri observed, dwelt on one of the coloured lithographs concerned with the romantic adventures of Genovia, the one showing the heroine being carried away on the charger of the marauding knight with her dress ripped open and her bosom exposed. The strong-man ate three bowls of *fasolia*, so that there was no second helping for Dimitri.

The strong-man, it appeared, intended staying only three days in Kalymnos. 'A wonder you don't go off your head in this dump,' he said to Nomiki. 'Why don't you make him take you to Piraeus? A good-looking woman like you....' He allowed the destiny of a good-looking woman like Nomiki to remain unexpressed, his eyes wandering to the picture of Genovia thrown over the back of the horse.

'It's all right here,' Dimitri said firmly. The marauding knight in the picture on the wall had no neck either. 'It's a good life.'

The strong-man shrugged. 'These sponge-boats?' He smiled at Nomiki. 'You come some time to Piraeus you look me up,' he said expansively. 'I got plenty friends there: you just ask anyone for Hercules.'

When he had gone, to settle about his hotel and to arrange his permits with the police, Nomiki said, 'What a nice man Mr Kudaris is!' and Dimitri nodded absently.

'He's so interesting.'

Dimitri nodded.

'And very polite.'

Dimitri nodded.

'He's very handsome, too.'

Dimitri nodded.

'And he did enjoy the *fasolia*, didn't he?' Nomiki smiled happily.

'He did, yes,' Dimitri said shortly, and went down the hill to his boat.

The strong-man's first demonstration was given that afternoon in the *plateia* that edged the crowded harbour. He was extremely voluble in explaining each of his feats, so that the performance was prolonged to the point where his final escape from the ropes and chains developed into a race against the accumulating dusk. Towards the end of the demonstration Dimitri observed his wife among the crowd in the front row. He pushed through to her.

'I was on my way home to eat supper,' he said pointedly.

'Have you ever seen a man as strong as Mr Kudaris?' Nomiki said breathlessly, as if she had not heard him.

'I was talking of supper,' Dimitri said patiently.

'Oh, we can have the *smarithes* cold.'

'From yesterday?' Dimitri said distantly. He was, in fact, rather partial to cold *smarithes* the day after they had been cooked.

Nomiki smiled up at him. 'We could have had the *fasolia*, but it was all eaten. Mr Kudaris liked it so much.'

'Come,' her husband said quietly. 'We will have the *smarithes*.'

He was still picking morosely at the platter of cold fish when the strong-man came to the door. He was carrying a flask of retzina, a basket of bread and cheese and oranges and dried octopus, and a bottle of sweet *mavrodaphni* which was obviously for Nomiki.

'We've eaten,' said Dimitri.

But neither the strong-man nor Nomiki appeared to have heard him. His wife began to spread the table with the flower-patterned cloth with the green silk fringes, the one reserved for feast days and for Sundays when special visitors called, and after the octopus had been smoked and dipped in lemon juice she hurried off to a neighbouring house to borrow a vase of flowers for the centre of the table.

While she was away the strong-man stared at the picture of Genovia, humming *Psarapoula* to himself, as if he was not interested in talking to Dimitri but was only killing time until his wife returned. Dimitri found himself ruminating on the absurdity of a man spending his life straightening horseshoes or biting nails in two. What earthly use was a *straight* horseshoe? Or half a nail?

'You ought to take a job with the sponge-boats here, Costas,' he said. 'Down there off Alexandria they could use a strong chap like you. That chest of yours, maybe you could dive seventy metres.' Dimitri, who could dive seventy-five, put the suggestion in a faintly challenging way, but the strong-man only shrugged and smiled and continued to stare at Genovia.

'Alexandria!' he said with startling disparagement when Nomiki returned. 'That's a second-rate circuit. Now Cairo, that's different.' He looked meaningly at Nomiki. '*There's* a town you should see, Cairo. Along Melika Farida, all those smart women . . . .'

Early on the following afternoon Dimitri climbed the hill to the house to pick up a new coil of rope he had bought for the boat, and to his astonishment there drifted from the kitchen the quite unmistakable aroma of beans stewing slowly in olive-oil. *Fasolia* was for Tuesdays, and this was Wednesday.

'*Fasolia*?' he said to Nomiki. 'We had it yesterday.'

'Mr Kudaris is coming to eat with us. It's what he asked for.'

'Ah.' Dimitri nodded. 'I meant to tell you, I'll be eating at Tony's *estatorion* with Vassilis and Constantine. There's *sikoti* and they've got a lobster.'

'Oh, that will be nice,' said Nomiki. 'You like *sikoti*.' She did not seem at all concerned.

'Maybe I'll put it off.' Dimitri frowned. It would be a lot of trouble, really, trying to arrange for the others to go to Tony's, and perhaps there would only be *fasolia* anyway, and it wouldn't be as good as Nomiki's. 'You better make a good lot,' he said darkly. 'That Costas, he eats like a horse.'

'Why do you always call him Costas when his name is Hercules?' Nomiki shook her head reprovingly. 'It's not good manners to always get names wrong the way you do.'

'I keep forgetting.'

Dimitri had a cheering thought when they were eating, and he said, 'So it's back to Piraeus again tomorrow, eh, Costas?'

But the strong-man shook his head and glanced rather significantly at Nomiki and said, 'No, no. I'm staying on another week or ten days. It's nicer here than I thought.' He ladled out another helping of beans. 'In Piraeus, where would I get *fasolia* like this?'

In the days that followed Dimitri arranged it so that he could spend as much time as possible around the shipyard at Lavassi, where all the caiques were pulled up on the slipways. There was plenty of work for him to do, splicing the new sheets and halyards on his own boat, the *Agios Stefanos*, and most of the other captains had jobs for him because he had a big reputation for handling ropes, and now that the winter overhaul of the boats was nearly completed there were all the finicky bits to be done: ends to be whipped and the lanyards and gear for the diving ladders to be ornamented with wonderful fancy knots and Turk's-heads.

But however industrious he was he could not help thinking about the corporal cook from Rimini who called himself

Hercules. On the Friday he had come again to eat with them, and this time Nomiki had cooked the *fasolia* in the huge shiny *casserolia* which, in the normal course of things, would be used only once a year, when they had the lamb for Easter. And on Saturday there had been nothing to eat at all, because the strong-man had taken his act to Chorio, the old village two miles up the valley, and Nomiki had gone to watch although she had seen all his performances and there was never anything new to them.

On this occasion Dimitri had gone back to the *plateia* and spent the evening drinking retzina with the men from his boat: it was quite late when he returned to the house and Nomiki was in bed and asleep. He had been too tired to awaken her. For a long time he sat on the chair by the side of the bed, just looking at her. It was not that he cared about her, he told himself, but he did resent coming back to an empty house and not finding his supper waiting. Although it would have been *fasolia* again, and he was becoming rather tired of *fasolia*. He was beginning to get a good deal of wind in the stomach.

'I'm not sleeping well,' he said to Constantine, who was crouched beneath the curved hull of the *Agios Stefanos* caulking the seams with oakum. 'I get a lot of trouble with wind.'

'I noticed,' Constantine said, a frown of concentration on his leathery face as he tapped the oakum into the seams with the long wedge-hammer. 'I hear you burping a lot. And you go red in the face.' He peered up from beneath the curve of the bilge. 'It's beans,' he said sagely. 'All that *fasolia*. *Fasolia*'s all right in moderation, but – '

'Nomiki makes the best *fasolia* you ever tasted!' Dimitri said with defiant loyalty. 'You're not going to say – '

'It don't matter who makes it,' Constantine retorted stubbornly. 'When it's beans it's always the same. There's a power of wind in beans. You ask anyone.'

It was on the Tuesday that Dimitri went up to his house early in the afternoon on the pretext of needing his palm-and-needle because the spare mainsail wanted patching. By the time he had reached the house he had practically convinced himself that it was nothing to do with the fact that the strong-man was back in town after a two-day tour around the other villages of the island, Vathý and Brosta and Myrtiés. Nomiki was sitting on the step in the sunshine, darning a hole in the sleeve of Dimitri's blue-and-white jersey.

Dimitri spent a considerable time in the kitchen pretending to look for the palm-and-needle, although he was perfectly well aware that it was in the box at the bottom of the kitchen dresser with his gut lines and fishhooks and sinkers. When he came out he said, quite casually, 'It is Tuesday, isn't it?'

'Tuesday, yes.' Nomiki looked up at him inquiringly.

'I just wondered,' Dimitri said blandly. 'I couldn't smell any *fasolia*, that's all.'

'But we've had so much of it, Dimitri.' She smiled. 'It's very upsetting if you have too much.'

'Tuesdays we always have *fasolia*,' he reminded her quietly, but with a measure of dignity, as the *papas* might remind her about attending Communion. 'I look forward to it on Tuesdays.'

She stared at him for a moment, a hurt, uneasy expression flickering in her large dark eyes. 'You've spoilt it now,' she said, smiling faintly, as if she might conceal her disappointment. 'It was to be a surprise. Mr Kudaris brought three kilos of *barbunia* back from Myrtiés. Lovely *barbunia*, caught off Telendos.'

'Ah, he likes *barbunia*, too?' Dimitri said detachedly.

'It's his favourite fish, Dimitri. And do you know what he said when he brought it up? He said . . . .' She hesitated and laughed a little self-consciously. 'He said: "Beans for strength, fish for sagacity, and a flower for a lovely lady."' She lowered her eyes, overcome by a sudden shyness, and she was flushing as she turned her head away. 'You hadn't even noticed it,' she said softly. Dimitri could see the rose crimson in her coppery hair.

The strong-man was only halfway through his act when

Dimitri reached the *plateia*. He eased himself to the front of the crowd and waited, curbing his impatience while the man continued with his interminable boring patter. The sun had already slid below the cliffs above Saint Vassilias by the time he came to his grand finale. He had borrowed a wicker chair from Katerini's *kafeneion*, and now he sat on it with his short legs wide apart and his fists on his thighs, and in a rather contemptuous way he was calling for a volunteer who might rope and chain him to the chair.

He seemed momentarily surprised when he observed Dimitri advancing towards him, but then he grinned and jumped from the chair and seized the opportunity of making another long rigmarole to the crowd. To the Greeks, Rimini is one of the brave names and the strong-man from Piraeus was by no means unaware of the magical power to loosen purse-strings that lies in an appeal to the things that are embedded in the militant heart of every true patriot. He talked of Rimini, of how proud he was that it was his old comrade-in-arms from that brave war who was to test his prowess: as he spoke it was in some curious way made to appear that it was the strong-man who had been decorated for gallantry while Dimitri had been somewhere behind the lines cooking macaroni. Dimitri, thoughtfully fingering the end of half-inch rope, testing its pliancy, appeared not to be listening.

Twilight was moving stealthily across the *plateia* when the strong-man returned to the chair and, with a knowing wink, motioned Dimitri to begin.

Dimitri went to the task slowly and with great care, beginning with a clove-hitch to the left wrist taken tightly to a double hitch on the back of the chair, a taut clove-hitch to the right wrist and then down to the thigh. The crowd was hushed and watchful and Dimitri, without looking up from his work, was conscious of the sailors and divers turning their heads and nudging each other and whispering together. Bowlines and sheepshanks, intricate hitches and reef knots; the special straining knot that old Lazarus the *colazaris* had taught him for making fast the big stone the skin-divers carried down to the seabed; and then a mesh of cunning interlockings ending in a final double clove-hitch that would have baffled Houdini. Dimitri wrapped the chain around the bound, rigid figure, but he did it carelessly as if, after the rope, it was the merest redundancy.

After he had done, Dimitri pushed through the crowd and had a leisurely coffee at Katerini's, and by the time he came back the dusk had settled over the *plateia* and the street lights had come on and the strong-man was still there, rigidly seated in the centre of the murmuring crowd. His complexion was much darker and his eyes were blazing and the veins on his throat and forehead were bulging out like cords. Like knotted cords. Dimitri walked over casually and examined the ropes but everything seemed to be holding. He glanced for a moment into the baleful eyes of the strong-man and then he looked away.

'That *barbunia*,' he said, 'it's not as good once it gets cold.'

The starry night had settled over Kalymnos when Dimitri left the *plateia* and began to climb, whistling softly to himself, towards the little blue house on the hill. As he climbed he could almost smell in his nostrils the warm grilling smell of *barbunia*.

At the top of the steps he looked down. The crowd had thinned out a good deal and people were still drifting away to their home and their suppers. Beneath the street lamps there were only a few men and a clot of delighted children around the writhing figure of the strong-man: and old Katerini, fat and infuriated, was slapping him over the face and shoulders with her dishcloth because he had broken the leg of her cane chair rolling around on the ground trying to escape. And in the stillness of the enclosing night a sound that was more than music drifted to the ears of Dimitri – the sort of bellowing and screaming you might hear when a hog-tied animal was being taken to the slaughterhouse. Dimitri went happily up the hill.

They ate the *barbunia* on the steps outside the house and Dimitri sighed with a deep content as he rubbed his bread around the bottom of the platter where, in the lamplight, the oil and lemon lay like a pool of molten gold.

'I still think we ought to have waited for him,' Nomiki said guiltily. 'It would have been polite.'

'Listen,' Dimitri spoke quietly, but with a reverent ecstasy as if he were commanding his wife to hearken to a choir of angels. From the bowl of darkness below a sound of howling came to them, thin and anguished.

For a while they sat in silence, and then Nomiki began to laugh softly. 'Dimitri, it wasn't really fair, you know,' she said. 'Those knots of yours. You're so wonderful with ropes.'

Dimitri nodded.

'And it was your fault, too,' she said earnestly. 'You brought him in the first place. And he only kept coming because of the *fasolia*. That's true, Dimitri.'

'No man comes that often for beans,' Dimitri said quietly. 'Not just for beans.' He shook his head. 'He kept coming because...because....' He hesitated and took a deep breath, the sort of breath he would take when the *colazaris* told him the next dive was on the deep shelves, seventy-five metres, maybe more. 'He kept coming because...because....' Dimitri moistened his lips. 'He kept coming, Nomiki,' he said bravely, 'because you are very beautiful.'

And he reached across the heaped platter of picked *barbunia* bones and took her hand in his.

THE VERDICT

*

by George Johnston

When he came out into Righillis Street he found the day brighter and bigger than he had expected it would be, as if the circle of sage-mauve mountains that surrounded the city had made a big effort while he had been inside and had shouldered the clouds higher. The heavy, handsome glass-and-iron door of the apartments where Doctor Georgaikis had his practice whispered behind him, folding the centrally heated air in after his departure with a soft click, furtive and secret like a stealthy footstep, as if there were something he was not supposed to hear. During the later hours of the day he would find himself smiling at this thought, but not yet.

All the marble and well-fitted glass and the angled balconies gave an opulent look to the apartments, and the flood of later autumn flowers cascading from the window-boxes added a nice touch of cared-for comfort; but the building faced an extensive vacant lot which was sordidly unattractive in this enlarged morning light. Trodden ramps of clay, half completed excavations which held yellow water from the rain of the night before, and abandoned shafts of reinforced concrete presented another disturbing aspect of the pervasive picture of Athens in transition. The black rods of the reinforcing steel writhed out of the concrete pillars like huge worms trying to release themselves and escape into the pools below. The parched, tingling smell of cement dust came at him on the cold, fitful wind, not from the vacant lot where not very much was happening, but from the new buildings all around where concrete-mixers were chattering and shovels were stirring thickly at the grey muckheaps, and diminutive men in shabby clothes were climbing ladders behind rough barricades of nailed-up planks covered with chalky dust. On some buildings whole façades were hidden behind huge screens of sewn sacking darkened by wet patches, but the dust still drifted.

Beside the ramp leading down to the vacant lot, where two desiccated pepper-trees trailed forlorn branches which smelt unsettlingly of his childhood, there was a bold sign which said, in Greek and English, *Parking Here For U.S. Mission Cars Only*. Even at this earlier-than-diplomatic hour there were nine or ten cars already there, arranged as neatly as chess pieces – the long sleek vehicles of a superimposed prosperity, with projecting fins like missiles, all very glossy, with the highlights touched in like the colour advertisements in magazines. At the edge of a clay bank sat a shabbily dressed gipsy woman, grimy flat feet splayed uncaringly in the dust. She was industriously wrapping in soiled rags the listless baby which would be her stock-in-trade during her day's begging around the streets and taverns. The woman was quite young and handsome enough, with sad, bold eyes and a kind of injured arrogance in the drape of the garish shawl, fringed and printed, that was flung about her shoulders.

She began her ingratiating whine of appeal as David Meredith came across the road and appeared, tall and bone-thin, at the top of the ramp, looking down at the shining cars. When this had no effect she spread her legs wider and shaped her body more insolently and called up to him an offer to tell his fortune. He smiled down at her and shook his head and walked away down the pavement towards a row of buildings ice-white beneath the fumed, dun-soiled sky above the Piraeus factories. Knowing his own fortune, he savoured the added irony of her offer. A flock of sparrows chittered up from the wasteland and flew off into the grubby sky above the white buildings. Birds flying off to the right. Another omen, he thought, adding to the irony.

He was aware that he had realised his own fortune from the moment he had seen that particular expression on the doctor's face when he had been admitted from the waiting-room. That little flick as of something being withdrawn and concealed, like a drawer being closed, or a hand laid across something written. And then that over-frowning, obviously pretended absorption in the papers on his desk, the artificial trick of patting at his pockets and testily pushing aside the piled-up trade bulletins and brochures from the drug houses, and muttering to himself as if there was something he had mislaid. So that his later injunction had been no more than a tentative, timid approach towards the instant of decision, backed away from at once.

'I shall want you to come back here this evening, Mr Meredith,' he had said, frowning again as if some other thought had abstracted his concentration for a moment. 'Come rather late, around eight, after surgery hours,' he had said in his precise, unaccented English. 'We'll want to have a talk. Yes, we can talk then. You see, I have seen the report from the clinic, but I have not seen the actual X-ray film, and I want to do that this afternoon. The film I *must* see, you understand? So around eight then, eh?' A smile then, swift and friendly, although his small pale blue eyes seemed still to search for the thing he had mislaid.

David Meredith turned along the street of ice-white buildings, which at a closer inspection proved to be dull in texture and more grey than white and marked by the vertical smudges of rain stains, and walked up past the Royal Palace to the thick green wall of the gardens where two Evzone guards in frilly skirts and white stockings and pompom shoes slow-marched and turned, balletic figures outside the toy props of the sentry-boxes. Their young dark eyes, as he passed, slantingly watched him from beneath their tasselled skull caps.

It was still only nine forty-five, so there were rather more than ten hours yet to be filled in, and he had no wish to go back to the cheerless solitude of the clean and cheap and quite impersonal little hotel room he had taken near the Tower of the Winds, where he had nothing to read except Faulkner (who would be discouraging as well as depressing) and *Moby Dick* (which he had already read more times than he could remember).

He felt an odd little twinge of wistful sadness that the island where he lived with Cressida and the children was four hours away from Piraeus by steamer: and, anyway, the *Nereida* sailed sharp at eight in the morning and by this time would already be past Aegina. At the thought of this the picture of his home at once gathered to itself the configurations of a dream, the white house blurred and brilliant with other white houses, the island set clear and rocky, a hallucination of solidity, in the dark bright run of the Aegean seas, lost beyond the smear-fume of the factories, beyond the grasp now of a considered reality.

A week had passed since he had returned to the island after that first careful, inquiring examination (why had the doctor needed to know that his mother's name was Minnie?), so that really there had been plenty of time for the man to have studied the reports of all the tests, and seen the X-rays, and talked with the radiologist and the microbiologist, and settled on his diagnosis. He could only be stalling now. Well, it was true that his waiting-room had been crowded with patients, meek-eyed and tractable, stolidly turning the pages of the German rotogravure magazines which none of them could read; and perhaps the evening was the appropriate time for a considered talk – for the verdict.

Ten hours. Meredith thought of the murder trials he had covered at the Old Bailey, before the time of expatriation, when he had been a newspaper correspondent in London. He had been intensely interested then, as a writer, in the intellectual subtleties of suspense, in the tensions and time-lags of jeopardy, of fates impending. It was a subject which had begun to fascinate him very much earlier, during the war years, especially in the jungle, where time and tension always moved on a thin green thread; and, later again, in China. Sometimes, at the Old Bailey, the jury had been out ten hours, or even longer, before they filed back to the box bearing gravity like a miraculous ikon, and the prisoner would be brought in and held there standing between two stiff, bulb-eyed policemen while the jury foreman recited the verdict in a voice scratched by solemnity. Well, now he would know something of what the prisoner had felt during all those ten slow-ticking delicately perfect hours, waiting to hear the decision. The thought gave him an odd little kick of pleasure: it had exactly the piquant flavour of his thought about the omens.

He walked on up past the Evzones' barracks to the wide bright plummeting shrieking traffic-rush of Queen Sophia Street, a tumult of nervous hurry beneath the sedate slow lift of the flags on the legations and the embassies, and he went down past the flower vendors to the square, where coffee tables were laid out neatly like a rare collection of postage-stamps hinged to the page of an album. Had he not been able to read Greek the fiery, neon-vivid letters of the advertising signs above the square might have served as a printed heading to the album page, with catalogue references and valuations in smaller print. Because of the chill wind blowing scraps of papers across the square and tugging at the artificial-looking oranges in the huddled trees, nobody was seated at any of the postage-stamp tables.

Meredith knew that if he sat out in the wind he would begin to cough again, but if he took a table right in the centre it was unlikely that a waiter would bother to cross all that blowing distance just to vend a three-drachma cup of coffee. He made a point of selecting a table exactly in the geometrical centre of the square, measuring with a careful eye the diagonals from corner to corner, and after his coughing spasm had passed he lit a cigarette and thought again of omens.

After he had wakened and showered and was dressing himself

for the appointment with Doctor Georgaikis he had pulled on his left sock first, which he remembered always having done as a child for the good luck of the day, and then, when he was lacing his shoes, he saw with subdued pleasure that he had put both socks on inside-out, which was of course a sign of particularly good fortune. He did not change them. Then, as he went out through the swing doors of the little hotel, the first thing he saw was a white horse, which was drawing a shallow, decorated little cart laden with potted plants and cut flowers to the flower stalls outside the church in the Plateia Agia Irini. He resisted the temptation to spit-wet his finger and mark a cross on the toecap of his shoe and to mutter the incantation, 'First luck, white horse!' – which as a child he certainly would have done – but, nonetheless, the incident gave him a sensation of great buoyancy.

Walking up Kolokotronis Street towards the old palace he made a careful point of dodging around two stepladders that straddled the sidewalk, feeling a sharp, agreeable sense of the superstitious as he skirted them. Near the end of the street a third ladder bridged the pavement, and as he approached it there was a tangle of traffic in the roadway, with a barrow-pedlar deep in vituperation with a taxi driver whose face was as red and militant as a flag, and Meredith decided audaciously to assert the intelligence of the rational man and walk boldly beneath the ladder. But when he came close to it he saw that four thin cords had been fastened between the rungs and the iron grille of a shop window, so that nobody could pass beneath the ladder anyway, and he had to pick his way around it, so that this particular sensation of compulsory participation in a superstitious rite gained a special subtlety and became deliciously meaningful and portentous. This, and then the gipsy's offer, and the sparrows flying off to the right . . . .

So far as Meredith was concerned there was a sardonic sort of quirk to all this. During his earlier years in China he had developed a particular interest in omens – the extreme sense of fatalism attached to Chinese gambling, the unsuperstitious attitude of the people towards death, and the practical eccentricities in the geomancy of *feng-shuei* notwithstanding – and this interest in the Oriental attitudes towards fatefulness had of course also taught him that the true absolutes of life were almost invariably ironical. This, at least, was what he had concluded. So that he had long since learnt to twist, as it were, all omens into reverse. Propitious signs became, to him, dark auguries, and the symbols of ill-omen were at once transformed into portents of personal benevolence. It was, in a sense, a sort of perverse intellectual game he played with himself.

Coming to Constitution Square through the bus-disgorged crowds of briskly hurrying office workers he therefore saw the sequence of small omens which he had observed since his awakening as a series of dark beads strung upon a thread which had, to him, a very familiar touch – a thread he had come to finger often in the last two years. He was absolutely certain he knew what the medical diagnosis would be. He was of the age for it, his chain-smoking and his nervous history gave it validity, and three of his best friends, all of them newspapermen, had died of it. In fact it had been the certainty of this knowledge which he possessed that had made him, until a week or so before, reject all Cressida's worried pleas that he should go up to Athens to see a doctor. In these refusals he had at first been careless and casual, then stubborn, and finally angry. Not until the discovery that he had dropped from an underweight one hundred and fifty-six pounds to an alarming one hundred and twenty-two had he surrendered to his wife's justifiable anxiety.

Now that the examination had become a *fait accompli*, and he harboured, like a precious secret, his own knowledge of what the finding would be, he had no feeling of alarm at all. Indeed, the sensation was rather one of elation and relief, of having come at last to the final resolution of a long and difficult problem. He felt exhilarated, and touched with an almost jubilant excitement. He felt at last like a man cleansed of misgivings.

No waiter came to the table in the middle of the square, and after a time Meredith changed his seat so that he could see, between the new airline offices and a jittery bright Telefunken sign, the austere columns of the Parthenon rising from the crumpled grey-pink rock of the Acropolis. It diverted him to recollect that he had once thought of writing a historical novel based on the life of the tyrant Peisistratus; and in a cluttered drawer in his little study on the island were the random notes he had put together with the thought that one day he might attempt a study on the last days of Pheidias, his trial and imprisonment, and the still lingering mystery of his death. He smiled to himself. The folly of these conceits amused him now. The chaste, saffron-washed columns remained up there on the rock, the virginal purity of thought cut in fluted stone, while twenty-five centuries of mortal ambitions, the big ones and the trivial ones alike, blew away like the cement dust in the air. And the novel he had begun to write about the journey he and Conover had made from Kweilin to Liuchow – that could be stuffed in the drawer also with all the other dog-eared papers. (Whatever happened, he wondered, to all the dog-eared papers that people left behind?) There was no point in trying to finish it now. He did not have to finish it because he no longer found it necessary to prove anything – either to himself or to anyone else.

When you came to think about it carefully, this of course was the basic reason for the extraordinary, weightless feeling of release. Release, yes, rather than relief. There was something enormously satisfying and soothing in the thought that he need not, would not, keep on trying, that tidal forces beyond his own control had drifted him into the calm centre of purposelessness. The books he had already published, mediocre as they might be, at least had some commercial continuity: for a year or two they would continue to earn royalties for Cressida – sufficient anyway for her to get herself re-established and make some arrangements about the house and the children. And the joy of it was that he would no longer have to try to tilt his blunted little lances at those windmills on the hill of contemporary writing. He could round it all off as an ex-newspaperman turned commercial novelist and let it go at that, with some garish covers on some inflammatory paperbacks and a little money coming in as insurance for his dependants, and to hell with delusions of literature and a remembered name. He was glad now that Cressida was the younger by eleven years; and she was capable and very attractive still. She would be all right.

Cressida. There was, he had to admit, a vague wrench of pain when he thought about Cressida. They had been married for a long time, thirteen years, and although in that period they had become very much habituated to each other, and from time to time had quarrelled with violence and even with hatred – there had been a snappish, bitter squabble in the doorway of the tailor's shop only the day before he had come up to Athens for the examination; sufficient for explosive recriminations and to reveal certain harboured resentments normally kept discreetly hidden in the locked cellar of self-control – even so there had been no time, really, when he had not loved his wife very deeply. The thought of living without Cressida had never, to him, been tenable: the prospect of losing her had occasionally (and without the slightest warrant, so far as he knew) racked him with nightmares of anguish, jealousy, and remorse. The queer feeling now, and this was a feeling so strange that his breath seemed to catch as if the acrid cement dust in the air had solidified his respiration, was that it was just as untenable to imagine dying without Cressida as to imagine living without her – both things, of course, being essentially parts of the same adventure.

Yet – a little catch of panic forced him to think it out more logically – it was clear that this element of release had to be examined as a mutual, not just a personal, thing. Over the last two years, since he at first, and she later, had been aware of his illness, there had been forces at work, only partially suppressed, forming subtle changes in their relationship. Very definite to see now, although nothing of it had been discussed, or even inferred. Future plans had never been considered in any very long-term perspective. His own restless, driving obsession with work – in that period of two years he had written three novels and begun drafting out a fourth – had been attributed to his passionate desire to produce something 'worth while' (the term they had used to define the windmills); and this in turn had provided a valid enough excuse for his almost constant state of nervous and physical exhaustion, and for his recourse each night to the stimulus of liquor. More important still, it ambiguously excused him from those sexual responsibilities which a husband normally owes to his wife, and, for that matter, to himself. They had agreed – they had read it in some book on writers' methods – that 'sex and creative writing seldom mix' (evidently on the grounds that the afflatus of inspiration, however dubious, is capable of acting as efficient deputy for the far less complicated organs of reproduction), without bothering to consider that brandy hangovers and creative writing seldom mix either. The truth of it was, of course, that he in his weakening physical condition had cringed away from any physical contact with her out of sheer fear of inadequacy and humiliation, loving her desperately yet afraid to touch her. The nagging corollary to this truth had been a thought which only now could he allow himself to consider dispassionately – that Cressida herself had had no desire whatever that he *should* touch her. Well, this was another problem that would be taken out of his hands now.

It was at this point in his reflections that Meredith was seized by a heavy fit of coughing, and he realised that the chill and gusty wind, with the deadening surroundings of all those unoccupied, postage-stamp tables, were beginning to give a depressingly dark tinge to his thoughts, to destroy those exhilarating nuances of self-examination which had so stimulated him on his walk back from the doctor's surgery.

He pushed back his chair and strode quickly across the square while the pigeons, fat and flightless as earthbound auks, scurried around his feet.

By the time he had put the square behind him the earlier temper of his mood had returned, and he went with buoyant step towards the old section of Plaka. Activity, he decided, was the keynote. He would walk round the city, with no more aim to his direction than a nostalgic drift towards remembered places. When he felt hungry he would get a *pita* with *souvlaki* and a mug of beer at some roadside stall: there were a hundred taverns and coffee-houses where he could rest over a glass of cognac or a beaker of wine. There were friends he knew in Athens, and bars where he would be certain of finding noonday company; but he had a profound wish to be alone with the new bright clarity of his thoughts.

In his queer mood of sharpened perception, the old section of Athens – this Athens which he still loved in spite of the new concrete monstrosities which everywhere intruded through the dust-screen of blowing cement – assembled itself to Meredith with a kind of limpid innocence, with the adventurous freshness of arranged toys, as if his was the unsullied eye of a childhood vision. As if for the first time really seeing, he delighted in the subtle blending of colour-wash over colour-wash on the crumbling walls in shabby streets, the white lace in dark cool windows, a spider's weave among the nettles, a tarnished knocker in the form of a turbanned head, a kindled fire beside a chipped pale door, a knife-blade stirring sparks from the spinning emery within a dark, recessive cave where flame bloomed balefully in chambers as mysteriously removed from the known world as Lascaux. He would stop to rub his finger along a

grooved edge of ancient marble surviving as a threshold, to
pick a feather from a crevice in a wall, to touch the nubbled
skin of a *frappa* in passing a fruit stall. Everywhere he walked he
had a heightened consciousness of the alert brown faces passing
and the vendors crying their street-songs – finding a particular relish in that one tray-bearing pedlar of spectacles who
shouted his tempt along the twisting streets, 'Glasses for long
sight and short sight!' – seeing the children absorbed by devices
in the dust or marking the cabalistic *graffiti* on the walls of a
library that had once been Hadrian's. Hoops bowling, tops
spinning, kites tugging, the bright, enclosed, sunwashed, brim-
ful streets awash with the running streams of life. Blue beads
on the necks of donkeys, the agate eyes of goats, and a cockerel
of beaten gold proudly pacing among the steam-pressed, ducoed
taxis. Shoes hanging in Pandrossou like the fruits of some strange
tree, and the dust and garlic and hot iron smell of Monasteraiki,
with the brass and copper gleaming in forge-lit darkness like the
old soft smoulder of an ikon.

Steadily and steadfastly he walked down the passing hours,
allowing side streets to beckon him to shops of odd employment,
the soldering of ancient bed-frames and the weaving of rushes,
and squares to tempt him to the gimcrack decor of the kiosks;
and it was not until the later afternoon, with a damp chill filling
the shaded streets and blotting up the colour of their detail, that
he realised how weary he had become. He found a table outside a
coffee-house on a busy street, and he ordered a double brandy,
but before the waiter had returned with it he had two unexpected visitors. The first was fear, and the second was Nitza,
and Nitza came tripping on the very heels of the swift, icy terror
that had afflicted him, and her spiky heels castanet-rapping
against the marble squares rhythmed the sudden staccato panic of
his heart.

He had known her less than well – a transient summer
visitor to the island whom he had distantly admired for her

beauty and vaguely envied for her youthful ebullience – but he grasped at her coming now with a desperate familiarity, springing to his feet and greeting her as if they were the most intimate of friends. She remembered him and responded with a smile that was warm enough, but at his request that she should sit and have a drink with him she shook her head reluctantly.

'I have to make a plane,' she explained. 'I'm on my way to the terminal now. I'd love to some other time. Some other flight maybe . . . .'

He remembered now – she was an air hostess . . . stewardess? . . . what did they call them? – on one of the Continental airlines. Which one? Olympic probably, since she was Greek. There had been a crash the day before in a storm over the Pindos. Everyone had been killed. The newspapers had been full of it, and those sickening grey pictures of torn earth and litter. It would not do to mention that, he reflected, desperate to find some point of conversation that would hold her, bring her to his table, seat her beside him.

'Come on, you must have a minute,' he said.

'It was one of our planes that crashed yesterday,' Nitza said brightly, and her eyes smiled at him. 'So we all have to be very perky,' she said. 'Couldn't afford to be late, you see. I'd love to some other time,' she said. 'I really would. I'd love to.'

She was gone with the same warm smile, the prickling quick clatter of her heels on marble rapping the cold little studs of fear into his heart. Left alone in the dimming cheerless light of the hurrying street he saw at once that there could be no tactlessness for Nitza in death or disaster – not with that youthfulness, that smile, that prettiness, that ebullience, not with the onward rattling of her high spiky heels to guide her.

He was cold now and afraid, and he felt very strongly his aloneness. He wished the waiter would hurry with the double brandy. The wind, stirred into chill eddies by the café corner and the overhang of awnings, touched him with a nervous sense of premonition. He wished she had stayed to talk to him, so that he would not have to think of the hour yet to pass, or of the lonely lights marking the silhouettes of buildings against a sky which had turned the colour of curdled cream, except in the west above the factory reek of Eleusis where it was growing dark and yellowish, like a bruise or something putrescent.

When the waiter brought the brandy he drank it at one draught, without bothering about the water, and dropped ten drachma in the saucer and got up at once and moved off into the packed flow of people and the dazzle of the neons and the skittery screech of traffic; and he had walked almost two blocks – and quite quickly, like the other people, as if there were some purpose behind it – before he realised that he was heading back towards Righillis Street. This brought him to an uncertain halt outside an arcade with a Chat sign where hairy rugs dyed in chemical colours were hanging beside a framed display of movie stills of a French film concerned with a teen-age problem. So for a moment or two the stripped girl and boy sharing a shadowed bed in the twelve-by-ten glossies and David Meredith were the only immobilities in a scurrying urgent environment of people with purpose.

He decided, since he was already on the way, that he might just as well set out for the surgery now, killing time, walking very slowly round the blocks, taking the long way. Movement was the only way of keeping the fears at bay: it was only when he sat down that the misgivings crowded in on him.

The Evzones outside the sentry-boxes were wearing blue now, dark-blue stockings and fustanellas and stocking-bands of black and cape-like jackets, not wearing white any longer. At some time of the day the season had changed, and he found this transition not only strange but jarring in some peculiar way.

Once he came to Righillis he made a point of walking down the wrong side of the street, casually sauntering like someone out for an evening stroll, stopping unnecessarily to look at the magazines and key-chains and plastic combs hanging from the cigarette kiosks, watching the reluctant poodles being cozened in the gutters; but even so it was still only seven-twenty when he got to the vacant lot with the clay ramp and the U.S. Mission sign. There were no cars at all in the parking lot. His eyes searched rather desperately for the gipsy woman, but there was no sign of her.

For a time he waited in the darkness beneath the pepper-trees, plucking at the soft green fronds and rubbing the pink, brittle-skinned peppercorns between his fingers, all the time looking across at the bright lights of the apartment building from which the flowers spilled now in colourless cascades, like black-and-white photographs of garden arrangements, and therefore unsatisfactory (he reflected) because the apartment building was like a glossy magazine really, and it was axiomatic with glossy magazines that garden arrangements, like food displays, could only be depicted in colour. Across the street at intervals the glass-and-iron door would open soundlessly and a figure would emerge and go quickly away along the dark street. He tried to wonder and to guess about these people, but his own fear too tightly encased his thoughts.

Eventually he began to walk up and down, deliberately taking fifty paces one way and fifty paces back; but he did this rather furtively, like some malcontent, and always kept within the thick darkness beneath the pepper-trees, until after five minutes or so he decided to change this tactic because he found himself wishing for one of two things – either that Doctor Georgaikis would come to the glass-and-iron door and stand there against the lighted shimmer of the rich marble and beckon him across, or that he and the shabby gipsy woman could find each other again. The gipsy woman had quite suddenly become more important than Nitza, or Doctor Georgaikis, or Cressida even – more important to him than anybody he had ever known. He began to move farther to the north and south along the ridges of the allotment, peering through the broken fencing and looking down the eroded banks of clay into the puddled allotment, searching in the darker places of shelter. But there was no sign of the gipsy. He had a bitter sense of anger and frustration that neither of his wishes was to be gratified: if there had been one of the sleek and shining automobiles in the lot, he told himself, he would find a big stone or a chunk of broken concrete and throw it at the bodywork, just to put a dent in it.

At twelve minutes to eight he crossed the road and went in through the bright door and rang the surgery bell, and the neat, quiet, motherly Greek nurse who admitted him bobbed an odd little deprecating curtsey, and there was a kind of nervous compassion in her eyes, as if she knew something she had been sworn to conceal. From the surgery he could hear muted talk and once the chink of metal against glass. There was nobody else in the waiting-room, and the talk went on behind the closed door and he had to wait for twenty-eight minutes in the smell of leather and glass and marble and pallid flowers and stale magazines and heated air, turning the German rotogravure pages without seeing the polished blonde faces, until a frightened looking little man of middle age with a peasant's moustache and an ill-fitting suit of black serge came out with his eyes bulging and was expelled by the motherly nurse through the sighing door: and there was Doctor Georgaikis with his short white jacket and his stethoscope beaming and beckoning him towards a bright cube radiant with white enamel.

'Yes, it is a quite undeniable tubercular condition,' Doctor Georgaikis was saying, examining without solemnity his own impacted fingers. 'But certainly not serious. Not these days. Slight shadow on the upper right lung, quite trivial really, an area rather more extensive high on the left lung. Nothing to worry about, I assure you, Mr Meredith. Drugs, rest, a little care . . . we can have you right in not much more than a matter of weeks. You've a good, tough constitution. No malignancy, thank goodness. A little care, peace of mind, rest — that's what you need. Now, what I *did* want to talk to you about was . . . well, getting some readjustments in your way of life. I'm afraid we shall have to do something about your smoking, *and* your drinking. And you must try to overcome your own tendency towards nervous stress. Peace of mind is what we are after . . . .'

When Meredith came out the sky was a swinging glitter of stars like powdered ice, and the street was deserted beneath the dark banks of the pepper-trees, and he walked very slowly across the road and down the clay ramp to the allotment. He did this with an appalling feeling that there was nowhere else for him to go, for he felt as heavy as the clay or the concrete columns and as desolate and empty as the place itself. For a long time he poked around the slopes of the ramp and he even walked along the wall to where a tumbledown shed huddled in a litter of broken struts and palings; but when he found that the gipsy woman was not there either he returned unhappily to the middle of the allotment and sat down on a mound of soil and shingles and stared down at a stagnant puddle of water in which star-sheen swam like tiny fishes.

The smell of the crushed peppercorns was still on his fingers, and it brought back all his childhood, and he knew that nothing had been resolved and that he had to begin all over again. He felt so miserable that he could have cried. He put his head down in his hands and wished that he was dead.

VALE, POLLINI!

*

by George Johnston

The Italian philosopher Pollini was born at the age of sixty-two years on the Greek island of Hydra on a bitterly cold March night in 1955. In a way, he came into the world more tempestuously than he deserved, for the man was a quietist at heart. Yet on that night in March a gusty sleet-laden *boreás*, blowing off the snow on the Peloponnese mainland and across the grey wild tumble of the Saronic Gulf seas, rattled the windows of Gregori's tavern on the waterfront and had us all huddled around an inadequate charcoal brazier with our backbones freezing.

Arch-enemy of Sartre and the existentialists, doughtiest of crusaders against the materialism of the twentieth century, upholder of a virtuous paganism, intimate friend of Rilke's widow, author of *Erasmus and the Lost Way, The Kingdom of Lack, Epicurus – An Old Death and the New Transfiguration*, etc., propounder of the complex system of metaphysics involved in his major hypothesis that 'to want is to need', Pollini crammed much brilliant intellectual achievement into his all-too-brief career, for he was dead before high summer had come to the island in that same year of 1955. (That he passed out of this world to a storm of Olympian laughter is a fact which he would, I think, have relished in his own particular way, and passed off with that characteristic philosophical shrug of his.)

There were, in the winter preceding the coming of Pollini,

173

only seven of us foreigners living on the island. (They can hardly be counted now, even off-season, but this was true then.) We were all expatriates trying to be creative people. The island at that time was stricken by neglect and poverty and was falling into decay. A house could be bought for almost nothing and rented for even less. Living was quite possibly cheaper than anywhere else in Europe. So were wine and cigarettes. There were very good reasons for our presence.

Boardman the painter, a Californian, was here with his wife. The Frenchman, André, working with a primitive kiln and quick-flaring pine-brush from the mountains, was experimenting with pottery glazes. We had Pat Corrigan, an Irish writer from Dublin; Jenny, who was a sculptress, from Iowa; Sara Carson, a very beautiful Australian girl then aspiring to be a novelist. And myself.

In the years that have passed since those better days I have been outstripped by most of the others, but at the time of Pollini's coming I was actually the one comparatively successful member of the group. I wrote suspense stories under a shamed pseudonym and novels which were pretty bad but which at that time I believed in and which were, at any rate, commercially published. I had even had a paperback reprint. Boardman at that time had nothing in the Museum of Modern Art, nor anywhere else: I seem to remember that he had not, in fact, sold a painting in ten years. Sara was labouring then on *Summer Solstice*, her first novel. Jenny had temporarily dropped sculpture for painting and was experimenting with a theory (later proved invalid) that Chinese art forms were applicable to the Greek landscape. Corrigan was writing short stories for the 'little' magazines of high repute which were inclined to pay for contributions – if they paid at all – on the honorarium system. André was slowly going out of his mind with the problems of his kiln, for any change of wind would fracture the pottery he was baking. The wind was for ever changing. (It was not until several years later, when the rich tourists began to come, that the little terracotta Mycenaean horses and tomb figures which he so expertly forged turned the old kiln into a quite lucrative thing.) But I was the only one among us then who was making any money at all to speak of by trafficking with the Muses.

Still, we were a compatible and contented and hard-working group that first winter, living, for the most part, on bean soup, *halvah*, bouillon cubes, sultanas, dry bread, goat cheese, and retsina, and enjoying stimulating arguments far into every one of the wild, wet, windy waterfront nights.

The upsetting intrusion into this world began some time in February, when a false spring had flung cascades of wistaria over the white walls and bombarded the town with explosions of almond blossom and carpeted the steep, stony hills with a million wildflowers.

It was a drift at first, but with a swift acceleration, so that before very long there must have been about eight of the new-comers sharing our tables in the taverns we favoured. They were all different, of course, but in some particular way they were also all the same. There were two Parisian existentialists (we did not have the word 'beatnik' then, or at least we had not heard of it in Hydra), a youngish Swede travelling with a load of neuras-thenia bigger than his rucksack, a Berlin youth who collected pornography, an American Negro called Brake who had lived for some precarious years in Munich, and three white Americans who were not physically all alike, but who had an astonishing similarity in the clothes they wore, in sexual propensities, and in the high skill they shared in the game of putting other people down intellectually. One, rather improbably, had been a taxi driver in San Francisco, with certain vice strikes against him. His name was Werner. Rather dark stories were told about the other two, Prosser and Fellbecker; or, rather, not told so much as hinted at. They were men who, having suffered dissipation for a long time, were ageing out of their thirties rather alarmingly. I still remember those tight, pinched lines around their mouths. We gathered that they were supported by small but regular remittances from the United States (the figure was usually put at a hundred dollars a month), and it was more than rumoured that these emoluments were conditional on their staying permanently and far from their own country. In Fellbecker's case there were sinister rumours of a wife mysteriously dead in Mexico and of certain inconclusive investigations. Prosser, in his cups and weeping, would sometimes give a blurred sort of significance to a never-very-clear tale of some bygone but still startling scandal in Philadelphia. They were completely 'Europeanised', for by this time they had both been expatriates for a good many years, during which their prowl had been the regular free-loader beat of Munich – Berlin – Paris – Majorca – Ibiza – Tangiers – Ischia. Greece, though, was a new experience for all of them, and they were quite candid in admitting that they had been lured not only by the cheapness of living and the expansive hospitality of the people but also by the moral tolerance of the Greeks. They had all known each other before, of course, at various points on the prowl.

The newcomers favoured tight blue jeans and either striped T-shirts or roll-neck sweaters, depending on the weather. All wore their hair very long except the young Frenchman, Jacques, who favoured the Roman fashion of the Caesar busts, and his mistress Francine, who wore hers cropped like a boy's. Jacques also wore one gold earring. Francine displayed the jawbone of a dog on a leather thong around her neck. (The French couple, being man and woman, as it were, had this sharp distinction from all the others in the matter of sexual predilection. Jacques, however, was faithful to a principle rather than to a person, and his eyes fell at once and contemplatively upon the delectable Sara.)

The striking thing about all of them was their apparently immense cultural erudition. In some mysterious fashion (by mail perhaps, for they were everlastingly writing or receiving letters: they lived poste restante, and often their letters came with as many as six or seven re-addressings) they seemed able to keep up with every breath of change and fashion in the intellectual climate of the world. They knew the latest reviews of all the best plays, books, movies, art show, ballet, music, and could even drop selected quotes from their favourite iconoclasts. They always knew who was 'in', who was 'coming', and who was slipping. They could – and would, in almost every conversation – quote in the most chastening manner from Gide, Proust, Rimbaud, Brecht, Mallarmé, Auden, Baudelaire, Henry James, Kafka, and Gertrude Stein. Also from Joyce, Lawrence, Sartre, and Beckett. And many more. They shared a vast fund of amusingly malicious personal anecdotes which pointed up their earlier intimate friendships with Auden, Picasso, Graves, Dali, Alice Toklas, Hemingway, Noel Coward, Nancy Cunard, Norman Douglas, Stravinsky, Dylan Thomas, and Rilke's widow. (Werner also had quite warm spots for Farouk and Gracie Fields.) Names like Hegel, Nietzsche, Heidegger, Kierkegaard, Marx, Jung, Freud, and Santayana dropped like cigarette-ends, with the relevant quotations, and all the casual aplomb of somebody asking for the salt to be passed. They also talked nonchalantly about the book they were writing, the volume of poems shortly to be published, the play being finished, or the one-man show of abstracts which had been fixed for the Galérie Rive Droite. (Their conversation was, in fact, the only evidence one ever had of these accomplishments or intentions, since they never seemed to move out of reaching distance of the post office.)

The fact remained that little more than a week of their company was almost enough to reduce the rest of us to a dismal recognition that we were nothing but a bunch of Goths and morons. Ignorant, inarticulate, intellectually barren. Sterile. Hopeless. They put us down, intimidated us, cowed us. They were condescending, yes, but we were never in doubt that they despised us, even if they did go to some pains to dissemble their contempt. There was, of course, a reason for this. To put us down, to blow away as so much cultural dust any self-confidence we might have possessed, this they felt to be necessary, and in any case the task to them was an enjoyable one. But to have displayed their scorn too openly would have been unwise, for here certain economic angles were involved, and these angles were not to be jeopardised by any over-rash or too-blatant assertion of their superiority.

I was in the somewhat curious position of being the main target for both their disdain and their economic acumen. I wrote a commercial 'slick' type of story, which in itself was hard to forgive: the fact that I was actually *published* put me quite beyond the pale. None the less, this was a bullet they had to bite on, and on the whole they did manage to veil their distaste, since I was about the only one with any money at all. They all drank very heavily. And somebody, after all, had to be left to pick up the bill, or to pay for their food in the taverns, or to 'hold them' until such time as American Express forwarded on their remittances. I laboured for a time under the delusion that if I lent them enough they would have to stop 'borrowing' from me because of shame at owing so much and not repaying it. It was only later that I saw my own naivety. They would have considered my paltry contributions as less than fair payment for their evangelical work of bringing culture to the barbarians.

There was the day Fellbecker came to the house, for instance, to borrow another hundred drachmas from me. He was particularly flattering that morning. He spoke of my 'solidity', assured me that I was 'all of a piece', and confessed rather wistfully to how deeply he envied a 'really *integrated* guy'. After I had given him the money I watched, unseen and morose, from the upper window as he went down the stairs to the courtyard. There he paused, turned his back very formally to the front door, stooped over rather in the manner of an ibis bending for a doomed minnow, broke wind with a sound like a burlap bag ripping, and went out through the front gate snorting his disgust. Prosser, on a more or less similar occasion, varied the gesture of contempt. Having stuffed the borrowed money into his jeans he simply made an unmistakably obscene gesture at the house and said 'Banality!' in a snarling tone that was both withering and audible. A further complication at this stage was that Jacques had abandoned Francine to a fisherman in the next village and was pursuing Sara Carson (who happened to be my woman) with a cocksure Gallic fervour and a supercilious disdain for our philistine concern.

It was into this exasperating and, indeed, undermining situation that Pollini came.

It was Boardman, I believe, who ventilated the issue. The seven of us were crouched in a huddled circle over the grey coals of Gregori's brazier on that frigid late March night, the other more recent arrivals having gone off somewhere to pick up sailors. The wind snarled at the night and thudded shutters. 'Say, we've got to *do* something,' Boardman said, in genuine distress. 'Those bastards are driving me nuts. Driving all of us. I can't work at all now. *You* can't work. None of us can work. We don't even have any talk any longer. Only *their* goddam talk.'

'Then it's quite simple,' said Pat Corrigan. 'We must introduce our own man. Not theirs. *Ours.*'

We all looked at him questioningly, but his thin Irish face had grown reflective, and he buried his head in his long pale bony hands. 'Pollini,' he said at last, after some thought. 'Yes. It has the cadence of a name half-remembered. Heard somewhere. It strikes a chord. Pollini,' he said experimentally. 'Acoustic associations are there, you see. Bellini. Puccini. Boldini. Bernini. Cellini. There is something about it that's in the ear, don't you see? *Pollini,*' he said again, mouthing the name, and then looked up at us. 'Luigi Gabriele Pollini,' he said carefully. 'He has the chair of philosophy at Bologna now. He was born at Padua, of course, in 1893 – so that would make him ... let me see ... sixty-two, wouldn't it? But he's been at Bologna for donkey's years. Highly respected. Did any of you come across that last book of his, *The Kingdom of Lack*? Terrific. It'll get him a Nobel, you mark my words.'

There was a pause, in which we all looked at him blankly, and then:

'He wouldn't accept it,' said Boardman, catching on. 'Not Pollini.'

'And why shouldn't he?' put in Jenny. 'Rilke's widow maintained he should have had it years and years ago. When he was pushing that Neopaganism movement. Lord, you can't say he wasn't an influence, can you? Or still is, for that matter.'

'I'm not thinking of that angle,' Boardman objected. 'It's the man himself. His own temperament and attitudes. His sense of integrity, if you like. Well, the great thing about the guy. I remember discussing Pollini's character with Tom Eliot. We were having tea together at his publisher's place, looking out over the trees in Woburn Square, only a year after Tom had gotten his own Nobel. It must have been late autumn, because I can still see that yellow mulch of soggy leaves squashed all over the pavements ....'

It came quite easily. Glibly, almost. We were able to do it just as well as they did.

Even so, it took quite a long time to get Pollini firmly established on the island.

Corrigan took over the biographical side, and, in thirty-six foolscap pages typed in single-spacing, meticulously detailed the philosopher's life from his birth in a Paduan slum alley, through the many vicissitudes of his childhood and early youth, to the colourful reckless days of his association with d'Annunzio, on to his interest in philosophy developing as a result of his friendship with Benedetto Croce (Pollini attached an almost mystical significance to the fact that Croce's first philosophical essay, *History Subsumed Under the General Concept of Art*, was published on the very day of Pollini's birth in 1893), and the jubilation of the young Paduan philosopher at Henri Bergson's excited reaction to his now-famous first essay, *To Want is to Need – An Examination of Intuition*, in which Pollini had found call for four separate and distinct meanings for the word 'exist' where Kierkegaard had been satisfied with only three. (Pollini retained something very close to worship for Bergson right up until the Frenchman's embittered death in 1941; he attached an almost mystical significance to the fact that Bergson had been born in 1859, on the very day on which Darwin's *Origin of Species* appeared.) Corrigan left nothing out: Pollini's romantic but ill-judged involvement with Berthe Lancelli the contralto; his reckless but heroic role with d'Annunzio's mistress of long years before, the great but aged Eleonara Duse; his long and unrelenting feud with Sartre; those wild controversies aroused in the Southern states during his second sensational lecture tour of the USA; the ceaseless barrage of polemics with which he harried the Fascist authorities from his quiet entrenchment within the walled cloisters of the University of Bologna; his long quarrel with the Vatican which would have brought about his excommunication but for the fact that at the critical moment Pollini was taken ill with pneumonia and half the population of the province of Emilia crowded to the University gates to read the bulletins on the sick man's condition; his long and affectionate correspondence with the Rilkes. It is perhaps a testimony to Pollini's life and character that the work was done with so much care and devotion.

Sara Carson's task (luckily she had worked for some time in the Mitchell Library in Sydney) was the compilation of the Pollini bibliography: his books, papers, essays, lectures, the several extant versions of the famous Milan Manifesto, the so-called 'commentaries', and even a detailed appendix of his letters; and also a complete list of his honorary degrees from and guest professorships at foreign universities.

My job was to develop a succinct precis of the main principles of Pollini's philosophy, his theories, postulations, and commentaries, critical analyses of his books, and a list of quotations from his writings to meet almost every foreseeable contingency.

Luckily, April came in with heat in the sun, warm enough to tempt Sara and me down to the sea rocks near the cave. By this time we were both feeling a need for relief from our long hours of scholarship, an hour or two of freedom, as it were, from Pollini, from the volumes of philosophy that littered my desk and the pages of plagiarism that bulged my folders. The day bubbled and sparkled like vintage champagne. The shadows of the cactus were dense and black against the crimson cliffs. It was one of the true times of the *halcyónë* and the gulls really did seem to be nesting on the blue milk of the peaceful sea.

But the rocks were under annexation and a transistor radio was playing. They were all there – Prosser, Fellbecker, Werner, Brake, Jacques, Francine, the lunatic Swede and the dirty-minded boy from Berlin – all there on the rocks, on *our* rocks, like a slime of stranded jellyfish.

'Oh God!' I groaned. 'Are they taking *this* over too?'

People always look so different with their clothes off. Prosser and Fellbecker, in their faded V's were flabbier than one had realised and they had sagging, rather mournful rumps and a quantity of bruises. On Francine the dog's jawbone as a striking feature took second place to the puckered scar of an appendectomy which marked like a fingerpost the salient area of her scant bikini. Werner and the Berlin boy, the one with bruises and the other with acne, were, with much giggling, pretending to practise judo holds. Only Jacques, among them all, was impressive. Chillingly impressive. His superb body glittered as gold as the ring in his ear-lobe. He had a token scrap of paisley around his loins and a wild caper flower between his teeth, and his eyes, cool in appraisal and torrid in intention, began speculatively to undress Sara.

'Let's get back to Pollini,' I muttered cravenly, and took her by the hand and led her away.

On the way back we called in at Boardman's place, an old derelict sponge-warehouse dignified by the euphemism 'studio'. There were several crayon sketches pinned to the crumbling, scaly walls, and from these Boardman was just working the final touches to a life-size portrait in oils.

'Well, it has to be from memory, of course,' he said, with a little shrug of deprecation. 'Sort of. What do you think, though? Not bad?'

'But...but it's absolutely *marvellous*!' Sara cried. 'You've caught the likeness perfectly. I mean it's *him*!'

We knew at once it was Pollini, of course. And the likeness really was remarkable. One still remembers the wild, untamed frizz of fox-pelt hair, the clear lined brow above the intensity of eyes like black olives, that great crag of a nose, the heavy, even rather sensuous mouth that yet had something of the tender mobility of a woman's, the two curious warts on either side of the deeply cleft chin which later we would always jestingly refer to as Scylla and Charybdis.

'Now those sons of bitches have taken over the sea,' I complained to Boardman. 'They're littered all over the rocks by the cave. We can't work. We can't talk. Now we can't swim, either.'

'Patience,' said Boardman. 'Remember Pollini's dictum. "Transvaluing is a concern of our full freedom, and is opposed to all cognitive attitudes." We must find comfort in that.'

'Comfort in what? What the hell does it mean?'

'How should I know?' said Boardman. 'I looked it up in one of your books. Some guy called Husserl. It sounded nice.'

We did the memorising and the rehearsals in Boardman's

studio, partly because the others, having dismissed Boardman as a quite penniless paint-slinger, had never troubled to find out where he lived, and partly because it was somehow comforting to work beneath the penetrating, intelligent gaze of The Master, framed now in slats of boxwood and honourably centred on the studio wall. Also Boardman always kept a wicker-covered flagon of brandy on hand.

The compilation of all the data had taken us two whole weeks of hard work. To fix it in all our minds and to thoroughly rehearse our roles occupied another ten days, and during this time André and Jenny turned out some twenty-odd small portrait busts of Pollini (taken from Boardman's portrait and sketches) in terracotta clay. The weather remained balmy and all the busts came out of the kiln unbroken. 'Each of us should have one,' said Corrigan. 'Later in the summer we should be able to flog the left-overs to the tourists.'

During this rehearsal period something happened which was temporarily disconcerting. There were two new arrivals, a young man and a young woman. The man, whose comparative immaturity was cleverly concealed behind an immense black beard, was the disconcerting one. He introduced himself crisply on the waterfront, with a stiff little bow and a Germanic click of heels.

'Carol Caliesch. Swiss. I am pleasured,' he said, and flourished a card at us. There was his name printed. And his calling. Philosopher, it said. Quite clearly in type two points larger than the word 'Zurich'.

The young woman was not introduced. I think eventually we learnt that her name was Vicki. She was simply the philosopher's moll. There is just no other definition. Dark, intense, de-sexed, plain, the thick accents of her native New Jersey carefully overlaid with a feigned Middle European broken English, she was both 'feed' and 'claque' to the Biblically-bearded Swiss. She was rehearsed, loyal, and adoring, with her breathless 'Oh yes!

Oh *yes*!' to his every observation on or quotation from Hegel or Kafka or Kant or Lorca. She always stood or sat very close to him, her eyes subdued into her flesh, her flesh into her dark and rather sweaty shirt, her feminine personality into a murmurous echo-box of approval and admiration.

They left us to find a cheap room. His handshake had the limpness and the slightly clammy unpleasant touch of a used church candle. He left me feeling very troubled, and that afternoon I voiced my misgivings to the others in Boardman's studio: 'Well, he *is* a philosopher. It says on his card. The minute we open our mouths he'll just shoot us down.'

Corrigan, however, had also met the Swiss, and was not in the least dismayed. '*Him*?' He snorted. 'Are you barmy? Holy Mary, Pollini will just eat him and spit the bones out! I mean, if Pollini can maul Sartre! *And* Wittgenstein . . . .'

Still, there must have been something inhibiting in the coming of the philosopher because that night passed without Pollini's debut, and so did the following night, and the night after. We were all indoctrinated, rehearsed, word-perfect, and we sat like mutes round the table while the names and quotations and the unstanched dribbles of their erudition dropped as the gentle rain from the lips of Prosser and Fellbecker and Brake upon the place beneath.

'As Rilke nicely put it, "I am nobody and always will be",' Prosser on the fourth night was saying cleverly, reaching for the ouzo, meaning us, of course, and not himself, and only quoting anyway just to put us down.

'Pollini always questioned that,' Boardman said with a deadly calm. We all sat up at once.

'Who did?' asked Prosser, startled.

'Pollini. He refers back to it in one of his letters to Rilke's widow. I guess you know it. Well, "*Ich bin Niemand und werde auch Niemand sein.*" Pollini refused to reconcile the non-existence of "nobody" with the infinite existence implied by "always".

185

Okay, he's got something. On the grounds of logical positivism, Pollini had to take a stand, I guess. Regardless of the verse.'

'Who was that?' Fellbecker asked with caution.

'Pollini,' said Boardman.

'Ah,' Fellbecker murmured guardedly.

'Like Occam's Razor,' Corrigan said with a grin. 'I've always thought Pollini was sharper, though.'

'Occam's Razor, yes,' said the Swiss philosopher. He spoke with very little conviction, but the girl sitting next to him whispered, 'Oh yes! Oh yes!'

We dropped it at that, and three nights passed before Pollini's name was mentioned again. Our confidence had been restored, so that this time it was we who took the initiative.

'Did any of you,' asked Sara, 'read Quintland's piece on Pollini in *New Comment*?'

'Oh, who the hell cares about Quintland?' said Boardman dismissively.

But I wanted to know, so I said, 'I'll bet anything you like it was anti-Pollini.'

'Of course,' said Sara. 'It's presented as a critical analysis of the book. Quintland maintains that it's nothing more than thinly disguised Communist propaganda. That it's politics, not philosophy – well, that Pollini's *Kingdom of Lack* is the whole of the Western world outside the Iron Curtain.'

'What absolute bollocks!' said Corrigan. 'Oh, the book's an allegory; but can't imbeciles like Quintland see that the *Kingdom of Lack* is man's own soul? Anywhere. *Everywhere*.'

'Not Quintland,' said Jenny. 'He can't see anything but red spots before his eyes.'

I thought that none of the others would have anything to say. Werner floated a blob of cigarette ash on a puddle of slopped wine, pushing it around with a toothpick. Fellbecker broke matchsticks on to the table. The philosopher was staring away into space, muttering something inaudible, and the girl beside him seemed to be trying to read his lips. It was Prosser who looked up carefully and said, 'You still have that magazine?'

'Sorry. Not any longer,' said Sara. 'I wrapped up the potato peelings in it. I rather felt that was about what it was worth. But you get *New Comment*, André, don't you?'

'Ah yes,' said André, shrugging. 'But my copy I stoke 'er in the kiln.'

'Too bad,' said Prosser, and looked away.

'*Tant pis*,' said André.

We had to be very careful in the days and nights that followed never to overdo it. The name of Pollini came into our discussions more frequently, of course, but always we introduced it deftly and only where it was warranted.

Boardman and Corrigan were enthusiastic and I think anxious for an all-out assault, but I was rather cagey about the opposition, especially Prosser and Fellbecker. On two separate occasions, when they called on me to borrow money, I noticed that each of them made a rather too studiedly nonchalant examination of what books were scattered around. Neither of them said anything, though. Still, Prosser was obviously a little distrait because he was almost at the bottom of the stairs before he remembered what he had come for and had to walk all the way up again to ask me for the money. This so delighted me that I pressed fifty drachmas on him, although I had sternly promised myself that this time he should have twenty at the outside. He looked quite dejected leaving the house and made no obscene gesture of any sort.

Two days later the philosopher called on me to see if I had a German-Greek lexicon – this was the pretext, anyways – but I had the feeling that he had come to talk about something which he could not quite get round to putting into words. I saw him looking at the little terracotta bust of Pollini which stood on the shelf above my desk.

'Pollini,' I said.

'Of course,' he said. 'A fine head. Distinguished.'

'Well, it's not all that good a likeness. They're just gimmick things you pick up for a few *lire* around Bologna. In Emilia they turn them out by the drayload. Tourists grab 'em, mostly. And students passing through, of course.'

It was that same night that Corrigan, with telling emphasis, decisively won an argument with the Swiss simply by referring to Pollini's attitude in the controversy with Bertrand Russell on intuitive pacifism.

It was hard to restrain them after that. Corrigan's view was that with all the detailed data in our minds, with a hundred Pollini quotations at our fingertips, with the man's whole life and character as vivid to us as if he really existed, with Boardman's splendid portrait there in the studio – the Grand Old Man of modern European philosophy looking down at his devoted disciples from that sombre, heavy, intelligent face – how could we fail?

I was still for caution, but in fact circumstances themselves forced an acceleration in the campaign. It was the opposition now who seemed intimidated. They dropped names and quotations less spiritedly and far less frequently. They were inclined now to listen warily where before they had dominated every conversation. All this, of course, made more room for Pollini. Indeed there was one night when Boardman was obliged to keep the conversation going for a whole hour. He handled it superbly, I must say, even though he had to ad lib a good deal of it, and he had the rest of us in stitches with his anecdotes about Pollini's charming but somehow grotesquely absurd love affair with the singer Lancelli.

That must have been a specially disconsolate night for the opposition – normally there were only reviews to be discussed, analogies to be drawn from the Pollini texts, or quotations allowed to fall partly around the littered tavern tables – and it had a distinct effect.

The despondency — uncertainty? suspicion? frustration? ... whatever it was — must have been contagious. Jacques, who for days had been gnawing dispiritedly at his lower lip instead of trying to get his leg under the table and rub it against Sara's, went on a violent drunk that night, tried to smash up a fishermen's tavern, got two teeth knocked out by an accommodating *gri gri* boatman, and went whimpering back to Francine. The police expelled both of them from the island the following day. Werner, Brake, the mad Swede, and the Berlin connoisseur went back to their sailors.

Only Fellbecker and Prosser and the philosopher and his moll doggedly stayed on with us. But the strain clearly was beginning to tell. They were for the most part taciturn and moody, disheartened, almost absent-minded in a way. There was even a night when Fellbecker paid for the drinks. Certainly he did it in a dull mechanical way, like a man hypnotised. But still he did pay. We were so delighted with Pollini at this stage that not only did we award him the *Prix de Rome*, we also sent in his nomination for the Nobel.

'I can't tell you how glad I am they've done that,' Jenny said.

'Done what?' I cued.

'Nominated Pollini for the Nobel Prize,' she said. 'They *must* give it to him, mustn't they?'

'Oh yes! Oh *yes!*' the philosopher's moll whispered breathlessly.

The climax came the very next night. Again Boardman had been obliged to move in to breach another dark and brooding lull in the conversation, and he was explaining to the philosopher, in the simplest terms, something of Pollini's theories on the nature of personal egotism. 'You see, he defends it,' said Boardman, 'on the basis that there is a natural intuition towards self-aggrandisement, whereas modesty, for example, is nothing more than an artificial and imposed convention.'

'Oh crap!' Fellbecker exploded suddenly.

Boardman turned to him slowly, his eyebrows raised.

'I disagree absolutely,' said Fellbecker angrily.

'Is that so?' said Boardman. 'Well, so do a lot of other people. Your buddy Sartre, for instance, would contend – '

'I'm not talking about Sartre,' Fellbecker snapped at him. 'Nor anybody else. I'm disagreeing with *your* cockeyed interpretation of Pollini's dialectic.'

'Why the hell are you anti-Pollini?' Corrigan came in rather aggressively.

'He's not anti-Pollini,' Prosser squeaked. 'It's just that your superficial approach to – '

'You keep out of this,' said Corrigan threateningly.

'Lay off it, Pat,' said Boardman. 'I want to hear what Fellbecker's got against Pollini.'

'I've got nothing against Pollini,' Fellbecker said stonily. 'I'm objecting to your half-baked interpretations. To hear you talk you'd think he was the only goddam philosopher who ever lived. Pollini! Pollini! Pollini! So all right. You rate him that high why don't you try, for God's sake, to get him *right*? The way you all talk you make like he's the *only* contemporary philosopher in Europe. And even if he were, don't you think we owe it to him to see that his message isn't garbled and tangled and twisted around into . . . into pap that any moron can swallow without discomfort?'

'You're all so *superficial*,' shrilled Prosser. 'That's what I said. You all – ' He broke off suddenly and stared at Corrigan. We all did.

He was peering across at Fellbecker and there was that glassy fixed intensity in his eyes that one normally saw only towards the end of one of the ouzo jags he would get on whenever he received a rejection slip. 'Pollini's message . . . pap for morons . . . Pollini's message . . . .' He mumbled the words thickly, and almost absently, as if everything had become too difficult to remember. His head sank slowly into his long thin hands, and there was an interval when he was quite silent and motionless, and then his shoulders began to shudder and jerk convulsively until all the glasses on the table were rattling, and he was gasping in a kind of strangled, choking way. He gave one snort, took a deep careful breath, raised his head, opened his mouth, and laughed. His eyes were streaming. His laughter bellowed and brayed at the ceiling. Boardman jumped up and reached a restraining hand towards him, but his arm fell helplessly among the dancing glasses on the table, and he began to laugh too. In seconds all seven of us were laughing: roaring, fist-pounding, gut-wrenching laughter that sent the table over and all the bottles and glasses and two chairs crashing to the floor; and everybody else in the tavern stared at the seven of us as if we were mad.

They all left on the steamer for Athens the following afternoon. They paid none of their debts, returned none of the books they had borrowed, and they did not even stop by the tavern to say goodbye or to have a final drink or to pick up the little terracotta busts of Pollini we had brought along for each of them. We were a little regretful about the busts, but even that didn't really matter. They had all gone.

All, that is, except the philosopher and his moll. They stayed on. They had begun a poetry phase, and Lorca was the boy, and they were reading *Blood Wedding* to each other. But the philosopher hadn't really caught on at all, because he stopped Corrigan outside the post office two days after the others had left the island.

'You have in your house the books of Pollini?' he wanted to know.

'No,' Corrigan told him curtly.

'Not? Some articles, perhaps? A treatise?'

'No,' said Corrigan. 'Pollini's dead.'

'Ah, but of course, yes. I am aware.' His lips showed pink through a gap in the black beard. 'But his books, they are available, no?'

'No. They cremated Pollini. In Bologna. All his writings were burnt with him. That was his wish.'

'So?' The philosopher seemed both surprised and a little crestfallen. 'Ah yes, this is sad,' he said. 'A great sadness. I think I stay here now all through the summer. I would much wished to have studied him more than I have done. A very interesting philosopher.'

'Yes,' said Corrigan. 'He was all that.'